THE PERFECT CRIME, ALMOST

OM KADAYAT

Dedicated to those who have ever felt the chill of fear, the thrill of mystery, and the warmth of friendship.

To the dreamers, the doers, and the detectives in all of us. To those who seek the truth, even when it hides in shadows. And to the readers who love untangling mysteries, this is for you.

Contents

Contents

Disclaimer

This is a work of fiction. Names, characters, places, and incidents are the product of the author's imagination or are used fictitiously. Any resemblance to actual events, locales, or persons, living or dead, is entirely coincidental.

FOREWORD

They say a perfect crime is one that is never solved. A crime so meticulously planned, so flawlessly executed, that it leaves no trace, no clue, no suspicion. A crime that defies detection, a puzzle with no pieces.

Few stories capture the complexities of the human condition as intricately as a murder mystery. The Darlington case stands as a epitome to the fragility of wealth, power, and the facades we construct to protect ourselves. When the veneer cracks, what lies beneath can be both terrifying and fascinating.

The story you're about to read is more than a tale of whodunit. It's a study of human nature—of ambition, betrayal, and the lengths people will go to protect what they hold dear. As the detective's investigation unfolds, we are reminded that the truth is seldom simple, and justice is rarely straightforward.

I am honored to introduce this work to you, a gripping narrative that not only entertains but also challenges the way we perceive morality and truth. Prepare to be enthralled.

PREFACE

The allure of a mystery lies not in the answer but in the journey. With each page, we peel back the layers of secrets, lies, and hidden motives to uncover the core of human nature—both its beauty and its darkness.

The story of the Darlington family's murder is one of complexity and contradiction. What seems clear at first glance soon spirals into a labyrinth of deceit and revelation. Through the eyes of our determined detective, we embark on a journey to untangle a web spun with precision, where every thread leads to unexpected truths.

This book is an invitation to delve into that labyrinth. It challenges you to look beyond the obvious and to embrace the thrill of discovery. As you turn these pages, I hope you find yourself not only immersed in the mystery but also reflecting on the nature of justice, loyalty, and the secrets we all keep.

Acknowledgements

I would like to express my sincere gratitude to the following people for their invaluable contributions to this book:

- My family and friends: For their support and encouragement, which has been a constant source of inspiration.
- My beta readers: For their honest and constructive criticism, which helped me to improve the quality of my writing.
- And finally, to the readers: For taking the time to read this book. I hope you enjoy it as much as I enjoyed writing it.

PROLOGUE

The rain lashed heavily that night, it was tempestuous night matched the mood inside the luxrious, sprawling estate of Darlington family. Seven prominent members of Darlington family along with other business associates gathered to celebrate 70th Birthday of patriarch Augustus Darlington. Champagne glasses clinked, laughter echoed,and secrets simmered beneath the surface. Who knew, by morning the mansion was a crime scene. A murder one cannot think of..A murder that shook the entire city.

Augustus a man whose opulence was the stuff of legends,lay sprawled across his glided dining table, his lifeblood staining the pristine marble with his throat slit bore silent witness to a brutal and sudden end. It was terrific to see a billionaire murdered brutally. His children and their spouses, once basking in sunlit warmth of inherited fortunes, now stood aghast. Their eyes were burning with a mix of grief, greed and chilling suspicion that ran deeper than blood.

I

The Darlington Dynasty

A man of formidable intellect and ruthless ambition, Augustus Darlington had built an empire that stretched across continents. From humble beginnings, the young Augustus, a mere child of ten, had a dream of great power and wealth. His journey was marked by calculated risks, strategic alliances, and a ruthless disregard for ethics. The Darlington dynasty was a tale of both grandeur and darkness. The family's wealth and influence were unbeaten, but beneath the veneer of luxury and success lay a web of secrets, betrayals, and deadly rivalries.

Following were the prominent members of the Darlington Family who were present at celebration :

- Evelyn Darlington, the cunning and ambitious daughter, was the apple of her father's eye. She possessed a sharp mind. Her thirst for power knew no bounds, and she would stop at nothing to secure her own legacy.

- Henry Darlington, the youngest son, was a dreamer, a stark contrast to his family's pragmatic nature. Married to a woman far above his station, he often felt overshadowed by his siblings. Yet, beneath his gentle exterior, a hidden strength and resilience lurked.
- Victor Darlington, the eldest son, was a man of tradition and duty. Married to the beautiful and enigmatic Ophelia, he was expected to carry on the family legacy.
- Samantha, Augustus's niece, a woman of mystery and allure, she had a knack for stirring trouble.

Along with these kinship relations, there were many ties of Darlington family.

- Dalton, the family manager, was a loyal servant, but his loyalty was tested as he became entangled in the family's complex web of deceit.
- Mr. James, the family lawyer, was a man of integrity, but even he found himself compromised as he navigated the murky waters of the Darlington family.
- Kyle Richardson and David Ferguson, two of Augustus's most trusted business partners . Their loyalty to the family was questionable, as their own ambitions threatened to overshadow their allegiance.

The cops arrived at the Darlington mansion shortly after receiving a call from Victor, Augustus's eldest son. The scene was grim, and after a meticulous inspection, the Sheriff stood silently, his face unreadable.

A junior officer approached him and whispered, "Sheriff, you're thinking about Vincent Kane, aren't you? Make the call."

The Sheriff smirked and pulled out his phone. Detective Vincent Kane was not an ordinary investigator. He was a man of shadows, his dark, piercing eyes seeming to strip away the defenses of anyone under his scrutiny. His rugged features spoke of a lifetime spent pursuing justice, but beneath that exterior lay a relentless intensity—a burning desire to uncover the truth, no matter the cost.

The Sheriff dialed Kane's number. Moments later, a reply came—not a call, but a text.
"I'm in New York. Will meet you in two days. Got the news about Darlington. Damien will be there anytime."

Damien Frost, Vincent Kane's closest associate, was already en route. Known for his sharp instincts and loyalty, Damien was indispensable in solving complex cases. While Vincent excelled at unraveling motives and strategies, Damien specialized in gathering and analyzing evidence, as well as keeping a watchful eye on suspects through his extensive network.

When Damien arrived at the mansion, he immediately began his investigation. He searched for the murder weapon, but it was nowhere to be found. Taking charge, he ordered all Darlington family members to vacate the premises. Augustus's body was sent for autopsy, and Damien meticulously combed through the mansion for any traces of the killer. Frustratingly, the scene yielded nothing.

With no immediate leads, Damien called Vincent to report his findings. Vincent's voice on the other end was calm but firm. "Halt the investigation for now. I'll be there in 48 hours, and we'll start fresh. In the meantime, make sure none of the family members or party attendees leave the city."

But fate had other plans....

Two days later, Damien was at the office, carefully reviewing Augustus's autopsy report when his phone buzzed. He answered swiftly.

"Damien, this is the Sheriff. Get to the new residence of the Darlington family immediately. The other six family members... they've been killed!"

Damien froze for a split second before grabbing his coat and rushing to his car. As he drove, his mind raced. Picking up his phone, he called Vincent.

"Vincent," Damien said, his voice tight, "it's happened again. The rest of the Darlington family—six of them—are dead."

Vincent's voice was steady, though a hint of tension cut through. "I just landed. I'm heading straight to the crime scene."

The tragedy had deepened, and the clock was now ticking faster than ever.

II

The Investigation

Damien arrived at the crime scene, his boots crunching against the gravel. As soon as the Sheriff caught sight of him, he yelled, "Where's Mr. Kane?"

The iron gate creaked open, and in walked a man wearing a well-worn leather jacket, faded jeans, and a battered baseball cap.

"He's here," Damien replied coldly.

The Sheriff turned to the newcomer. "Mr. Kane, you were supposed to be here earlier! There's chaos everywhere. The Darlington family is famous worldwide, and I'm being hounded by the government. They keep demanding updates on this investigation. What am I supposed to tell them? That Mr. Kane was too busy in New York to show up? That we'll start investigating when he finally decides to grace us with his presence? Is that it?"

Vincent Kane calmly removed his cap, brushing dust from the brim before replying, his tone measured but firm. "First of all, Sheriff, Vincent Kane is not officially assigned to this case. Neither is Damien Frost. Yet he's been handling it for two days—at my request, mind you. Secondly, I work

360 days a year. If I take a five-day break, you and your government can survive without me. Now, let me ask you something: What have you done so far as the Sheriff? Anything? No? Thought so. Now that I'm here, let's get started."

The Sheriff, fuming, turned on his heel and stormed off without another word.

Damien shook his head. "Vincent, let's not waste time on him. I haven't seen the bodies yet. Let's head inside."

Vincent nodded, his expression unreadable, and followed Damien into the crime scene.

Vincent and Damien moved methodically through the estate, their footsteps echoing in the heavy silence. As they uncovered each scene, the weight of the Darlington family's grim fate pressed down on them.

Evelyn, Augustus's cunning daughter, was found slumped over her vanity table in her ornate bedroom. The faint scent of almond lingered in the air—cyanide, undoubtedly. A delicate teacup sat nearby, its contents a lethal trap.

Henry, the calm and youngest son, had met a brutal end. His body lay at the bottom of the estate's pool, tethered to a stone weight. The rippling water above him now stilled, carrying an eerie stillness that seemed to amplify the cruelty of his death.

Margaret, Henry's wife, had fallen victim in the grand ballroom. A shattered chandelier lay strewn across the polished floor, its jagged shards sparkling like a grotesque mockery of beauty. Blood pooled beneath the debris, telling the story of her fatal misstep.

Victor, the eldest son and the family's head in Augustus's stead, was found in his office downtown. His lifeless body slumped in his chair, the unmistakable marks of strangulation around his neck. Papers were scattered across his desk, as if he'd struggled to reach for help before the end.

Ophelia, Victor's wife, was discovered in the wine cellar. She lay amidst shattered bottles, her lips pale and tinged with blue. A broken wine glass rested near her outstretched hand, the air thick with the pungent scent of spilt wine and suffocation.

Finally, Samantha, Augustus's estranged niece, was found locked inside the garden shed. Her body bore signs of a violent struggle—bruises and gashes marring her skin, dried blood staining her clothing. The tools surrounding her seemed to mock the helplessness of her plight.

Vincent and Damien stood in silence, taking in the sheer brutality and precision of the murders.

Damien broke the silence, his voice heavy. "This isn't just a massacre. This is... calculated. Each one of them was killed in a way that reflects something about who they were."

Vincent nodded grimly, his expression unreadable but his sharp eyes scanning every detail. "A message," he murmured. "Someone wanted these deaths to speak louder than words."

The two men exchanged a glance, their mutual understanding unspoken but clear. They were up against something far darker than either of them had anticipated

The news of the billionaire family's tragic demise sent shockwaves through the nation. As soon as the news broke, a swarm of media outlets descended upon the crime scene, transforming serene estate into a chaotic hub of activity. News helicopters hovered overhead, capturing aerial footage of sprawling property cordoned off by the police tape. Reporters, photographers, and camera crews jostled for position, desperate to capture any glimpse of investigation. The air crackled with sound of live broadcasts as news anchors delivered breaking updates to a captivated audience. Social media platforms were flooded with speculation and theories fueled by the constant stream of news coverage. The detectives and Sherrif's deputies burdened with the weight of case, navigating through the throng of journalists.

After meticulously examining the crime scenes, Vincent issued a series of precise instructions to Damien. Once the orders were set in motion, the two men walked the perimeter of the sprawling estate, searching for any overlooked clues.

The residence was unnervingly pristine—too clean. It was as though the murderer had anticipated their every move, leaving behind no tangible evidence. They searched for notes, messages, or any hint of motive, but their efforts yielded nothing.

The bodies were promptly sent for autopsy, their gruesome stories now in the hands of the medical examiners.

"Damien," Vincent began, breaking the silence, "do you have any suspects?"

Damien sighed, frustration edging his voice. "I considered every possibility, even among the family members. But, unfortunately, nothing fits. It's as if the answers are just out of reach."

Vincent's expression hardened, his mind already racing ahead. "We're not chasing ghosts. There's a connection here—I can feel it. All these murders are tied together. We need to interrogate everyone who attended the birthday party. Someone there knows something."

Damien nodded, trusting Vincent's instincts. Without another word, they left the crime scene and headed straight to their office, determined to unravel the web of secrets surrounding the Darlington family.

Vincent's office was a chaotic masterpiece, a reflection of his mind. Stacks of paper, half finished coffee mugs. A corkboard, covered in photographs, newspaper clippings, and cryptic notes, dominated one wall, a visual representation of his ongoing investigations.

The Darlington family's estate manager, Mr. Dalton, sat stiffly in the interrogation room, his fingers nervously interlocked. Vincent leaned forward, his piercing gaze locking onto the older man's eyes.

"Mr. Dalton," Vincent began, his voice low but commanding, "Augustus was found dead the morning after his birthday. You've been the estate manager for this family for twenty long years. Naturally, you were present at the party. I need you to tell me everything—every single detail. Nothing is too small or insignificant."

Dalton cleared his throat, shifting uncomfortably in his chair. "Everything seemed fine," he started. "The party went smoothly. Augustus was in high spirits; he even organized a grand feast for the servants and security staff. After the feast, he instructed them all to leave and return the next morning. When the party ended, only seven members of the Darlington family remained in the mansion, along with the family lawyer, Mr. James, the family doctor, Dr. Marx, and two business partners—Kyle Richardson and David Ferguson."

Vincent tilted his head slightly. "Go on."

Dalton hesitated before continuing. "Well, during the evening, there was an argument between Kyle and David. Something about investments—nothing out of the ordinary for them. They always had minor disagreements, so I didn't think much of it at the time. "

Vincent's expression darkened, and he interrupted sharply. "Wait. You said everything was fine, but now you're mentioning an altercation? That hardly sounds insignificant."

Dalton fumbled for words. "It's just... well, they argued frequently. It wasn't unusual, so I didn't think it was worth mentioning."

Vincent's voice turned cold. "Let me make this clear, Mr. Dalton. You don't decide what's important—that's my job. Your responsibility is to provide every detail, no matter how trivial you think it is. Now, elaborate on the reason for this altercation. What exactly were they arguing about?"

Dalton swallowed hard, realizing he had no choice but to comply. "It was about an upcoming startup. Agustus wanted funding from Kyle and David but both of them denied."

Vincent leaned back, his sharp eyes never leaving Dalton. "Interesting. Keep going, Mr. Dalton. Leave nothing out."

Damien walks in 'Vincent, autopsy reports are here' Vincent then asked Dalton to leave for now.

Vincent and Damien settled into their chairs, the autopsy reports spread out across the desk. The room was silent except for the faint clinking of Vincent's coffee cup as he took a sip.

Damien broke the silence first. "The causes of death vary, as expected. There are struggle marks on everyone's body—except Augustus. But that's no surprise; at seventy, he wouldn't have been able to put up much of a fight."

Vincent nodded thoughtfully, his gaze fixed on the report. "I see. There's no consistent pattern to these murders. If this were the work of a serial killer, we'd expect a specific method of killing—a signature. But this..." He gestured at the reports. "This was deliberate. Each death was unique."

Damien leaned back, arms crossed. "Maybe the killer wanted to throw us off. Keep us chasing shadows."

"Possible," Vincent replied, setting down his cup. "But it's not just about creating confusion. This feels... personal. These weren't random acts of violence; they were tailored, almost like messages."

Damien nodded, though his expression remained grim. "One thing's for sure—we don't have the full picture yet. The DNA results should help, but those will take about a week to come in."

Vincent's eyes sharpened, and he leaned forward. "I'm aware. And I have a strong instinct about those results, Damien. When they come in, they're going to give us the breakthrough we need."

The two men exchanged a determined glance, the weight of the case heavy between them.

III

Veil of Suspicion

The air in Vincent Kane's office was thick with tension. The corkboard, cluttered with photographs of the Darlington family and their closest associates, seemed like a labyrinth of secrets. Vincent leaned back in his chair, his dark eyes scanning the web of connections. "Damien," he began, his voice calm but commanding, "let's start with the lawyer, Mr. James. If anyone knows the skeletons in this family's closet, it's him."

The Lawyer's Testimony:

Mr. James, a man of impeccable dress and polished demeanor, sat across from Vincent and Damien. Despite his calm exterior, beads of sweat glistened on his forehead.

Vincent leaned forward. "Mr. James, you're the Darlington family's legal confidant. Surely, you must know something about their personal and financial affairs that could help this investigation."

Mr. James nodded, adjusting his tie. "I do, Detective. But my relationship with the Darlingtons was strictly professional. Augustus was a shrewd businessman. He never let anyone get too close."

Vincent's eyes narrowed. "Were you present at the party until the end?"

"Yes," Mr. James replied. "I left shortly after Augustus gave his toast. I saw nothing unusual."

"Did you notice any arguments or suspicious behavior?" Damien chimed in.

Mr. James hesitated. "The altercation between Augustus and his business partners was... heated. But such disputes were common."

"And you didn't think it important to report this earlier?" Vincent's voice sharpened.

Mr. James sighed. "I didn't think it was relevant. Kyle and David argued with Augustus often. It was part of their dynamic.

Next, Kyle Richardson and David Ferguson were summoned. The two men entered the room, their expressions a mixture of irritation and apprehension.

"Kyle, David," Vincent began, his tone icy, "you both had a public disagreement with Augustus at the party. What was it about?"

Kyle crossed his arms. "Augustus wanted us to invest in his latest venture—a ridiculous gamble. We refused. That's all."

"And you left the mansion after the argument?" Damien asked.

"Yes," David interjected. "We left together. I dropped Kyle off at his hotel and returned to mine. You can check the CCTV footage and hotel records."

Vincent nodded. "We will. But tell me this—did either of you see or hear anything unusual before leaving?"

Kyle shook his head. "Nothing. The family seemed as dysfunctional as ever, but that's no surprise."

Evidence and Elimination :

Back in the office, Damien handed Vincent a report. "CCTV footage confirms Kyle and David's alibi. They left the mansion together and didn't return."

Vincent frowned. "What about Mr. James?"

"Clean," Damien replied. "No evidence linking him to the murders. His timeline checks out too."

Vincent ran a hand through his hair. "We're running out of leads."

Damien leaned forward. "But what if this isn't about the outsiders? What if it's someone within the family or their inner circle?"

Vincent's eyes darkened. "It's possible. But whoever did this is exceptionally cunning. They've left no trail—yet."

A Chilling Revelation :

Just as Vincent was about to call it a day, his phone buzzed. It was a message from the forensic lab: DNA results will be expedited. Expect them in three days.

Vincent shared the news with Damien. "If this killer made even one mistake, those DNA results will reveal it."

Damien nodded. "Until then, we keep digging."

The shadows around the Darlington tragedy grew deeper. Each clue seemed to lead to a dead end, but Vincent Kane's intuition told him the truth was closer than it appeared.

IV

The Manager's Shadow

The city skyline shimmered in the distance as Damien paced Vincent Kane's office. The room, lit by the warm glow of a desk lamp, was a chaotic landscape of documents, photographs, and notes pinned across a corkboard. The Darlington family case was as twisted as the history of the family itself.

Damien's voice broke the silence. "Dalton is the key. He was the last one to leave the party. If anyone had the chance to execute this murder, it's him."

Vincent didn't respond immediately. His sharp eyes scanned the evidence board, connecting dots in his mind. "Dalton has been with the Darlington family for two decades. He knows their secrets, their routines, their weaknesses. But loyalty doesn't rule out motive."

The sudden vibration of Vincent's phone caught both detectives to attention. He glanced at the screen. It was a message from the forensics lab: "DNA results are ready."

The DNA Revelation :

At the forensics lab, the atmosphere was tense. The lead forensic scientist, Dr. Linda Hargrove, met them in the analysis room, holding a thick file. She wasted no time getting to the point.

"We've completed the DNA analysis," she began, flipping through pages of data. "We found two distinct profiles on all the Darlington family members, including Augustus. One is unidentified—it doesn't match anyone in the family, nor is it in any known database."

Vincent leaned forward. "And the other?"

Dr. Hargrove hesitated, as if considering how to deliver the bombshell. "The other profile is a match for Thomas Dalton, the estate manager."

Damien's jaw tightened. "Dalton? Are you absolutely sure?"

"Positive," Dr. Hargrove confirmed. "Dalton's DNA is on every victim except Augustus. It's not enough to place him as the killer, but it's incriminating."

Vincent's expression hardened. "Unidentified DNA suggests an outsider, but Dalton's presence on the victims makes him a prime suspect—or a pawn."

Interrogating Dalton :

Dalton arrived at the precinct under a cloud of suspicion. The confidence he had displayed during his first interrogation was now tempered by unease. Vincent wasted no time.

"Mr. Dalton," Vincent began, his tone razor-sharp, "you told us you left the estate after ensuring everything was in order. So, how do you explain your DNA being found on six murder victims?"

Dalton's face paled, but he tried to maintain composure. "I—I don't know! I worked closely with the family for years.

My DNA could've been transferred from objects or casual contact."

"Don't insult our intelligence," Damien interjected, his voice rising. "Your DNA wasn't just near the victims—it was on them. That's a big difference."

Dalton stammered, "Maybe someone's framing me! I had nothing to do with those murders. I loved that family!"

Vincent's piercing gaze didn't waver. "Loved them enough to betray them? To profit from their deaths?"

Dalton's hands trembled slightly as he gripped the edges of the table. "I had no reason to kill them. Augustus trusted me. I managed everything for him—his estates, his finances. If I wanted money, I had access to it without... this."

Vincent leaned forward, his voice low and dangerous. "You said you locked up after the servants left. Did anyone else enter the house?"

"No!" Dalton exclaimed. "It was just the family and their guests—Mr. James, the family lawyer, and Dr. Marx, their physician. They were still inside when I left."

Damien narrowed his eyes. "And the altercation with Kyle Richardson and David Ferguson? What were they arguing about?"

Dalton hesitated before answering. "Investment disagreements. Augustus wanted them to fund a startup, but they weren't interested. They left shortly after the argument."

Vincent studied Dalton's face, searching for cracks in his story. "You're hiding something, Dalton. If you're not guilty, prove it. Tell us everything."

Dalton's voice rose in desperation. "I've told you all I know! If you think I killed them, arrest me. But you'll be chasing the wrong man."

Vincent leaned back, his expression unreadable. "For now, you're free to go. But don't leave town."

A Hidden Passage :

As Dalton exited the interrogation room, Damien's phone buzzed. It was an officer stationed at the Darlington estate.

"Detectives," the officer said, his voice crackling over the line, "we've found a hidden passageway in the mansion. It connects the east wing to the wine cellar. There are fresh footprints inside."

Vincent's mind raced. "The killer didn't need to enter through the front. They had access through the passage."

At the Estate :

Vincent and Damien arrived at the Darlington mansion as dusk fell, casting an eerie glow over the sprawling estate. The officer led them to the hidden passage entrance, concealed behind an ornate bookshelf in the study. The air inside was damp and stale, the stone walls lined with cobwebs.

Damien crouched to inspect the footprints. "They're larger than Dalton's shoe size. Definitely not his."

Vincent nodded. "This ties to the unidentified DNA. The killer—or killers—used this passage to move unnoticed."

As they emerged from the passage into the wine cellar, Vincent's sharp eyes caught something glinting under a barrel. He retrieved it—a small, engraved medallion.

"Damien, bag this. It could belong to one of the suspects—or our mysterious intruder."

Piecing the Puzzle :

Back at the precinct, the detectives reviewed the new findings. The hidden passage explained how the killer moved, but it didn't exonerate Dalton. The medallion was sent for analysis, and Vincent turned his attention back to the DNA report.

"Dalton's DNA ties him to the victims," Vincent said, sipping his coffee. "But the unidentified profile complicates things. This wasn't a one-man job."

Damien nodded. "If Dalton's involved, he's either the mastermind or a pawn. Either way, he knows more than he's saying."

Vincent tapped his pen against the table, deep in thought. "The medallion might give us a lead. Until then, keep a close watch on Dalton. If he's guilty, he'll slip."

A Chilling Theory :

As the night deepened, Vincent stared at the corkboard, the threads of the case weaving a dark web . "What if the unidentified DNA belongs to a hired killer? Someone with no ties to the Darlington family, brought in to do the dirty work?"

Damien frowned. "And Dalton helped them? Or was coerced?"

Vincent's eyes narrowed. "That's what we need to find out. Dalton's DNA makes him complicit, but the killer's identity is still in the shadows."

The hidden passage, the unidentified DNA, and the medallion hinted at a larger conspiracy. But in the world of power and deceit, nothing was ever as it seemed.

V

The Medallion Revelation

The early morning sunlight filtered through the blinds in Vincent Kane's office, casting long shadows across the room. Vincent sat at his desk, absently drumming his fingers on a pile of case files. Damien entered, holding a slim, sealed envelope from the forensic lab.

"The results for the medallion just came in," Damien announced, his tone both eager and cautious. He handed the envelope to Vincent, who tore it open with a precision born of impatience. His sharp eyes scanned the report.

DNA Match: Kyle Richardson.

Vincent tossed the report onto the desk, leaning back in his chair. "Kyle Richardson. The business partner who had an argument with Augustus at the party."

Damien nodded. "Makes sense, right? Maybe the argument escalated after Dalton left, and Kyle snapped."

Vincent shook his head, his instincts already whispering dissent. "It's not that simple. The DNA on the medallion places him at the scene, but does it connect him to the murders?"

Damien crossed his arms, a skeptical frown forming. "We know Kyle left the party after the altercation. If he returned, it would explain the medallion. Let's bring him in."

Interrogating Kyle Richardson :

Kyle Richardson was a sharp-dressed man in his mid-40s, his tailored suit and polished demeanor suggesting a life spent navigating boardrooms and high-stakes deals. He sat across from Vincent and Damien in the interrogation room, his expression one of irritation rather than fear.

"This is ridiculous," Kyle said, leaning back in his chair. "I've already told you everything I know. I left the Darlington estate after the argument. I didn't go back."

Vincent slid the medallion across the table. "This was found in a hidden passageway inside the mansion. Your DNA is on it. Care to explain how it got there?"

Kyle's confident face faltered for a moment before he expressed himself. "That medallion was a gift from Augustus. I wore it to the party. I must have dropped it somewhere."

"In a hidden passage?" Damien asked, his tone skeptical. "Seems like an odd place to lose something so valuable."

Kyle's irritation turned furious . "I don't know how it ended up there! Maybe someone picked it up and planted it to frame me."

Vincent's voice was calm but cutting. "And who would want to frame you, Kyle? You and Augustus had a very public disagreement about an investment. That's motive."

Kyle leaned forward, his voice rising. "Yes, we argued. But I walked away, like I always do. Augustus was stubborn, but he wasn't worth killing over a business deal."

Vincent studied Kyle's face for any sign of deception. "If you didn't go back to the mansion, why is your DNA the only match we've found so far?"

Kyle threw up his hands. "I don't know! But if you're trying to pin this on me, you're barking up the wrong tree. Run whatever tests you need—I didn't kill anyone."

The Lab Results: Another Dead End

Hours later, the forensic lab delivered additional reports. Damien skimmed through them as Vincent poured himself another cup of coffee.

"The medallion ties Kyle to the scene," Damien said, flipping pages, "but his DNA doesn't match the unidentified profile. And the footprints in the hidden passage? They don't match his shoe size either."

Vincent's frustration was evident as he slammed his coffee cup onto the desk. "So, we've got nothing. Again."

Damien leaned against the desk, trying to sound optimistic. "We know he was at the mansion longer than he claims. Maybe he saw something—someone—and he's hiding it."

Vincent rubbed his temples, the weight of the case pressing down on him. "Or he's telling the truth, and the real killer is still out there, laughing at us."

Damien with a smile on his face "Maybe the killer be as stressed as we are"

Vincent "As if you know him"

Laughing Damien " I think you know him"

A Growing Web of Questions :

The case was turning into a maze of contradictions. Vincent stared at the corkboard, his sharp eyes darting between the photographs and notes pinned in mess . Each clue seemed to point in a different direction.

Dalton's DNA tied him to the victims but didn't explain the hidden passage. Kyle's medallion linked him to the scene but left gaps in the timeline. The unidentified DNA remained the only constant—a mystery sneaking in the shadows.

Damien spoke, breaking Vincent's musing. "If Kyle didn't match the unidentified DNA or the footprints, who does? The medallion doesn't place him in the act of murder, but someone used that passage."

Vincent exhaled sharply, his frustration boiling over. "Every lead we chase brings more questions than answers. Dalton's lying, but he's not the mastermind. Kyle's connected, but not enough to arrest him. And the unidentified DNA... it's the only real thread we have, but it's leading us nowhere."

Damien hesitated before suggesting, "What if we're looking at this wrong? What if the killer is someone completely outside our radar? A professional?"

Vincent shook his head. "No. The killings are personal. Each victim was targeted in a specific way. This isn't the work of a stranger—it's someone with a grudge, someone who knows the Darlington family and their dark secrets ."

A Grim Reflection :

As the day turned to night, Vincent sat alone in his office, the flickering light of the desk lamp casting shadows on the walls. The Darlington case had become an intricate puzzle, each piece refusing to fit.

He replayed the details in his mind: Dalton's evasiveness, Kyle's medallion, the hidden passage, the unidentified DNA. The answers were there, buried beneath layers of lies and misdirection.

Vincent's thoughts were interrupted by Damien's voice from the doorway. "You okay, boss?"

Vincent didn't look up. "We're missing something, Damien. Something crucial. And until we find it, the killer stays one step ahead."

Damien nodded. "We'll get there. We always do."

But as Vincent stared at the evidence board, he couldn't shake the feeling that time was running out—and that the truth, when it finally surfaced, would be darker than he could imagine.

VI

The Shadows of the Past

"The funeral is going to be held tomorrow" Vincent told Damien. Damien replied "Well tomorrow I'm revisiting the hidden passage I might get lucky to find a clue, so I won't be showing up in funeral"

The next morning, The somber mood at the Darlington estate was interrupted by an unexpected arrival. As mourners gathered for the funerals of Augustus Darlington and his family, a sleek black car pulled up to the estate. Out stepped a man in his late sixties, tall with piercing blue eyes that mirrored Augustus's. Beside him stood a poised woman, her silver hair tied in an elegant bun, her expression unreadable.

Whispers rippled through the crowd as the couple approached the estate. They were Augustus's estranged younger brother, Charles Darlington, and his wife, Isabella. Their appearance was a shock to everyone, as the couple had been absent from the family's life for decades.

Vincent Kane observed the scene from a distance, his sharp mind already piecing together possibilities Vincent's eyes narrowed and whispered "Every time we think we've unraveled this family's secrets, another layer shows up."

A Curious Introduction :

Charles and Isabella were standing near the edge of the crowd when approached. Vincent extended his hand. "Vincent Kane. I'm leading the investigation into the Darlington murders."

Charles shook Vincent's hand firmly. "Charles Darlington. And this is my wife, Isabella. We flew in from Switzerland as soon as we heard the news."

"Switzerland?" Vincent added "That's a long way. Forgive me for asking, but why haven't we heard of you until now?"

Charles's jaw tightened. "Because Augustus and I had a falling out over thirty years ago. We cut ties with the family. But that doesn't mean I didn't care for him."

Vincent's eyes flicked to Isabella. "And you, Mrs. Darlington? Did you share your husband's estrangement?"

Isabella's voice was calm but cold. "I supported my husband's decision. Family disputes can be... messy."

"Messy indeed," Vincent replied, his tone neutral. "Would you mind if we asked you a few more questions? Standard procedure."

Charles nodded reluctantly. "We'll cooperate in any way we can."

Damien's Discovery :

While Vincent interviewed the newcomers, the investigation continued. Damien revisited the hidden passage with a team, determined to find more clues. As he combed through the narrow space, a glint of gold caught Damien's eye. He crouched and carefully picked up a strand of long, silver hair tangled in the crevices of the wooden floor.

He bagged the hair and sent it for immediate DNA analysis, hoping it would provide the breakthrough they desperately needed.

The DNA Results :

By late evening, the DNA results arrived. Vincent and Damien sat in their office, the tension evident as Damien opened the envelope.

"The DNA from the hair matches Isabella Darlington," Damien said, his voice tinged with disbelief.

Vincent leaned back in his chair, processing the information. "Isabella. She claimed to have supported Charles's decision to cut ties with the family. Yet, her DNA places her inside a hidden passage in the Darlington estate—a passage she shouldn't have known about."

Damien flipped to the second page. "But here's the twist: her DNA doesn't match the unidentified profile."

Vincent's brow furrowed. "And Charles?"

Damien pointed to another section of the report. "No DNA match, but his shoe size matches the footprints found in the passage."

Vincent stood abruptly, pacing the room. "So, we have Isabella's DNA and Charles's footprints in the same passage. One was there physically, the other left a mark. But neither matches the unidentified DNA, which means..."

Damien finished the thought. "They weren't alone."

Interrogating the New Suspects :

Vincent wasted no time in questioning the Darlington newcomers. Charles and Isabella sat across from them, their expressions a mix of indignation and unease.

Vincent placed the DNA report on the table. "Mr. and Mrs. Darlington, your estrangement from the family is no longer the most intriguing detail about you. We found traces of both of you in a hidden passage at the estate. Care to explain?"

Isabella's face hardened. "I don't know what you're talking about. I've never been in any hidden passage."

"Your DNA says otherwise," Damien countered. "We found your hair there."

Charles's demeanor shifted, his tone defensive. "We've been in Switzerland for years. We had no reason to visit the estate."

Vincent leaned forward, his eyes boring into Charles. "And yet, your shoe size matches the footprints found in that passage. You expect me to believe that's a coincidence?"

Isabella folded her arms. "Perhaps someone is trying to frame us. Given the family's history, it wouldn't surprise me."

Vincent tilted his head, studying her. "Framing you would mean someone knew about your existence. No one here even mentioned you before today."

Charles's voice rose. "We came here out of respect for my brother. Not to be accused of murder."

Vincent's gaze didn't waver. "Respect doesn't explain why your traces are in places they shouldn't be. If you're innocent, you'd better start talking—because someone in your family wasn't so respectful."

The Frustration Deepens :

After hours of questioning, Vincent and Damien had more questions than answers. Charles and Isabella's denials were firm, but the evidence placed them closer to the scene than they admitted.

Vincent stared at the corkboard in his office, the web of connections growing ever more tangled. Dalton, Kyle, Charles, Isabella—the pieces of the puzzle were piling up, but none fit cleanly together. The unidentified DNA remained a shadow over the investigation, a silent witness to the crime that refused to reveal its secrets.

Damien broke the silence. "What if they're telling the truth? What if someone really is trying to frame them?"

Vincent's frustration boiled over. "Then who, Damien? Who has the means, the motive, and the opportunity to manipulate every clue we've found?"

He slammed his fist onto the desk, the sound echoing in the room. "We're chasing ghosts, and every step forward feels like two steps back. This case is a labyrinth."

Damien placed a reassuring hand on his shoulder. "We'll figure it out. We always do."

Vincent sighed, his anger giving way to exhaustion. "The truth is there, Damien. Buried under layers of lies and deceit. But the deeper we dig, the more it feels like the Darlington family is a black hole, pulling us into their chaos."

As the night deepened, Vincent resolved to keep digging—because somewhere in the darkness, the killer was watching, waiting, and perhaps even smiling at their struggle.

VII

The Weight of Shadows

Detective Vincent Kane sat alone in his dimly lit office, a glass of whiskey in his hand and the Darlington case files spread out before him. The room was a chaotic collage of papers, crime scene photographs, and notes scrawled in his jagged handwriting. On the corkboard, a tangled web of connections stretched across photographs of the Darlington family and those surrounding them. Red strings crisscrossed in a maddening pattern, each one a potential lead that had spiraled into a dead end.

The clock ticked ominously, its rhythm only amplifying Vincent's mounting frustration. He pinched the bridge of his nose, his dark eyes closing as he leaned back in his chair. The weight of the case pressed down on him like an iron vice. It wasn't just the complexity of the Darlington murders—it was the history, the secrets, the lies. And, deeper still, it was the unshakable echoes of his own troubled past.

The Haunting Past :

Vincent had always been a man of shadows, shaped by a childhood he'd rather forget. His father, a failed musician, had drowned his disappointments in alcohol, and his mother had been a silent sufferer, enduring her husband's rage in stoic silence. The Kane household had been a battlefield of broken dreams and muffled screams. Vincent, the youngest of three siblings, had spent countless nights hiding in a closet, listening to the chaos unfold outside.

One night, the chaos had reached its crescendo. His father's anger had turned deadly, and by dawn, Vincent's mother was gone. Taken. Lost. The police had called it a domestic accident, but Vincent knew better. He'd seen the rage in his father's eyes that night, the coldness as he'd turned his back on his own children.

Vincent had vowed then and there to fight for the truth—no matter how painful, no matter how buried. It was a promise that had propelled him into law enforcement, but it was also a curse. Every case he took on brought him closer to his own demons, and the Darlington case was no different.

The Burden of the Case :

The Darlington murders were unlike anything Vincent had ever faced. Each piece of evidence felt like a taunt, a breadcrumb leading to more confusion. The DNA mismatches, the hidden passages, the estranged family members—it all seemed designed to frustrate him, to mock his quest for clarity.

Damien Frost walked into the office, a steaming cup of coffee in his hand. "You look like hell," he said, placing the cup on Vincent's desk.

Vincent offered a humorless chuckle. "That's about right. This case... it's like trying to solve a riddle where the question keeps changing."

Damien sat down across from him, his expression sympathetic but determined. "You've cracked tougher cases, Vincent."

Vincent shook his head. "This one's different. It's not just about a murderer. It's about a family so twisted that even their secrets have secrets. Every time I think I'm close, something else unravels."

He gestured to the corkboard. "Look at this mess. Dalton, Kyle, Charles, Isabella—their motives are all plausible, but nothing sticks. And that damn unidentified DNA... It's like a ghost, haunting every corner of this case."

Damien leaned back in his chair. "What about the Darlington siblings? Evelyn, Victor, Henry—they all had their fair share of enemies. Maybe this isn't about the family's secrets but their connections."

Vincent sighed. "Maybe. But even their deaths don't make sense. Poison, strangulation, drowning—it's like the killer wanted to confuse us."

Damien nodded. "It's working."

A Moment of Weakness :

As the night dragged on, Damien left to follow up on a lead, leaving Vincent alone with his thoughts. He stared at the photograph of Augustus Darlington, the patriarch whose empire had spanned continents. Augustus's face was stern, almost cruel—a man who had built his fortune with ruthless ambition.

Vincent saw shades of his own father in Augustus. The same relentless drive, the same coldness. He wondered if Augustus had ever shown his children the kind of warmth and care they deserved. Or had he, like Vincent's father, been consumed by his own demons?

His mind drifted to his siblings. His older brother, Michael, had followed in their father's footsteps, becoming a man of rage and regret. His sister, Caroline, had escaped, carving out a life far from the chaos of their childhood. Vincent hadn't spoken to either of them in years.

The whiskey burned his throat as he downed the rest of his glass. He rubbed his temples, feeling the familiar pang of guilt and regret. He'd buried himself in his work for years, but the ghosts of his past always found a way to resurface.

The Turning Point:

Damien returned with a new set of reports, breaking Vincent's spiral of self-reflection. "I've got something," he said, placing a folder on the desk.

Vincent opened it, his eyes scanning the contents. "What is this?"

"Financial records," Damien replied. "Charles and Isabella's accounts. They've been moving large sums of money over the past six months. Could be innocent, could be something else."

Vincent frowned. "Anything connecting them to the unidentified DNA?"

Damien shook his head. "Nothing yet. But there's more. The Darlington estate's security logs show a series of undocumented entries in the months leading up to the murders. Someone was accessing the property without authorization."

Vincent's frustration flared. "And we're only finding this out now?"

Damien shrugged. "The logs were buried under layers of encrypted files. Took our tech guys a while to crack it."

Vincent slammed the folder shut. "So we have secret visitors, estranged relatives with questionable finances, and a hidden passage no one admits to knowing about. And yet, no clear suspect."

He stood, pacing the room. "Damien, this case is a goddamn labyrinth. Every lead we get feels like it's designed to pull us further from the truth."

Damien watched him quietly. "You've been through worse, Vincent. You'll get through this."

Vincent stopped, his shoulders slumping. "I'm not so sure this time. This case—it's not just about finding a killer. It's about untangling decades of lies and betrayals. And every step we take feels like it's dragging me back into my own past."

Damien stood, placing a hand on Vincent's shoulder. "You're not alone in this. We'll figure it out. One piece at a time."

Vincent nodded, though his doubt lingered. The Darlington case wasn't just a test of his skills—it was a battle against his own demons. And as the shadows deepened, he couldn't shake the feeling that the truth was slipping further from his grasp.

VIII

The Relentless Pursuit

The Darlington mansion's shadow loomed over the investigation like a silent witness, guarding its secrets with eerie tenacity. Detective Vincent Kane, fueled by a mix of frustration and determination, decided it was time to intensify his efforts. With the new revelations about the suspicious financial transactions and the lingering questions surrounding the estranged relatives, he knew there was no room for hesitation.

Turning Up the Heat: The Manager and the Estranged Relatives

The following morning, Vincent and Damien summoned Dalton, the long-serving estate manager, along with Augustus's brother Charles Darlington and his wife Isabella. The interrogation room, stark and suffocating, felt like a pressure cooker ready to explode.

Vincent began with Dalton, whose loyalty to the Darlington family had come under serious scrutiny.

"Dalton, explain these transactions," Vincent demanded, tossing a folder filled with copies of the bank statements onto the table. His voice was sharp, his gaze unrelenting.

Dalton adjusted his tie nervously, his fingers twitching. "These are legitimate transfers. They were meant to handle estate expenses. The Darlington family runs a vast network of properties and businesses."

Vincent leaned forward. "Don't insult my intelligence, Dalton. These amounts don't align with routine expenses. Care to explain the six-figure sums sent to an unregistered account in Zurich?"

Dalton's face turned pale. "I—I was following orders."

"Whose orders?" Vincent snapped.

Dalton hesitated, beads of sweat forming on his brow. "Mr. Augustus," he finally stammered. "He wanted those funds moved discreetly."

Vincent's voice turned icy. "Convenient, isn't it? The one person who could verify your story is dead."

Charles and Isabella Under Fire

After grilling Dalton, Vincent turned his attention to Charles and Isabella. The couple, who had arrived from Switzerland under the guise of attending the funeral, now faced mounting suspicion. Their sudden appearance and connections to the Darlington legacy were too convenient to ignore.

Charles, a man with a wiry frame and an air of arrogance, sat stoically as Vincent hurled questions at him. "You expect us to believe that after decades of estrangement, you just happened to show up after the murders? What's your angle, Charles?"

"My angle?" Charles said, his tone cool and calculated. "Augustus was my brother, Detective. Regardless of our differences, I had every right to attend his funeral."

Vincent smirked. "And the unexplained financial transactions tied to your name? What's your explanation for those?"

Charles's eyes flickered with irritation. "I have investments, Detective. Not everything revolves around your obsession with this case."

Isabella, sitting beside him, interjected, her voice soft but firm. "We've been living a quiet life in Switzerland. We had no part in this madness. The DNA evidence may link me to the hidden passage, but that doesn't prove anything."

Vincent's patience thinned. "It proves you were there, Isabella. What were you doing in that passage?"

"I don't know," she said, her eyes narrowing. "Perhaps someone is trying to frame us."

The Breaking Point: Interrogation Turns to Torture

Days turned into weeks as the interrogation escalated. Vincent's frustration boiled over, leading him to employ more aggressive tactics. Long hours under glaring lights, psychological pressure, and relentless questioning took their toll on Dalton, Charles, and Isabella. Each interrogation session left them more exhausted but no closer to breaking.

"Dalton," Vincent growled during one session, "you've been at the center of this family's affairs for decades. You know every secret, every hidden corner. Tell me what you're hiding!"

Dalton's voice cracked as he replied, "I've told you everything I know! Augustus had his secrets, yes, but I wasn't privy to all of them. I did what I was told!"

Damien, observing from the corner, whispered, "Vincent, we're hitting a wall here."

The Narco Test: Truth or Deception?

As a last resort, Vincent ordered a narco-analysis test for the trio. The process, designed to bypass their defenses, was meant to uncover the truth hidden beneath their composed exteriors.

Dalton went first. Under the influence of the drug, he repeated the same claims: he had transferred funds at Augustus's request, but he knew nothing about the murders. "I swear," he slurred, his eyes half-lidded. "I didn't kill anyone…"

Charles followed. His responses were curt and consistent, even under sedation. "I was in Switzerland," he murmured. "I came back for the funeral. I… didn't… kill them."

Finally, Isabella underwent the test. Her voice, tinged with fear, echoed through the room. "The passage… I found it once… by accident… But I never hurt anyone."

Despite their altered states, none of them confessed to the murders. Their stories, while frustratingly vague, remained consistent.

The Aftermath :

The results of the narco tests left Vincent and Damien at a standstill. While the tests didn't exonerate Dalton, Charles, or Isabella, they also didn't provide the smoking gun Vincent had hoped for. The trio's steadfast denials under both interrogation and sedation only deepened the mystery.

Vincent sat in his office, the weight of the case pressing down on him like a stone. He stared at the corkboard, its tangled web of connections mocking him. The unidentified DNA profile remained a phantom, its origins a maddening enigma. The footsteps in the hidden passage added to the confusion, tying Charles to the scene but failing to reveal his role.

"Damien," Vincent said, his voice weary, "we're chasing ghosts. Every lead we follow just takes us further from the truth."

Damien placed a hand on his shoulder. "We'll figure it out, Vincent. We always do."

Vincent nodded, but his confidence wavered. The Darlington case had become more than just a test of his skills—it was a battle against the secrets and shadows that threatened to consume him. And for the first time, he wondered if he was losing.

IX

The Unyielding Shadows

Vincent Kane sat in his dimly lit office, the walls closing in around him. The once-chaotic masterpiece of photographs, red strings, and cryptic notes now seemed like a maze without an exit. Every lead he had chased had either looped back into obscurity or dead-ended entirely. The Darlington case had become his obsession, yet the answers remained maddeningly out of reach. Damien entered quietly, carrying a stack of freshly printed reports, his expression mirroring Vincent's exhaustion.

"Here's everything from the bank analysis, forensic updates, and background checks," Damien said, setting the pile on Vincent's desk. "I hope something in here points us in the right direction."

Vincent nodded wordlessly, his fingers already flipping through the papers. As Damien settled into the chair across from him, the air was thick with unspoken frustration. The weight of the Darlington family's gruesome demise hung over them like a storm cloud.

The Financial Web :

The first report Vincent scrutinized was the comprehensive bank analysis. Months of financial transactions from Augustus's accounts revealed layers of complexity, but nothing incriminating. Payments to overseas consultants, transfers to holding companies, and investments in obscure startups littered the statements. Each line item raised questions, but none provided definitive answers.

"Look at this," Vincent said, pointing to a set of transactions. "Augustus funneled over $10 million into a trust just days before his death. The beneficiary is anonymous."

Damien leaned over, squinting at the document. "Could this tie back to Dalton? He managed the estate."

"Possible," Vincent replied. "But Dalton's alibi is solid, and the narco test didn't shake his story. If he's lying, he's doing an excellent job of it."

"What about Charles and Isabella?" Damien asked. "They had access to the estate, and their connection to the hidden passage is undeniable."

Vincent exhaled deeply. "Charles's footprints match the passage, but there's no direct evidence linking him to the murders. Isabella's DNA complicates things, but again, it's circumstantial. We're running in circles."

The Forensic Labyrinth :

The forensic updates offered little solace. The unidentified DNA profile remained a ghost, appearing on multiple victims but refusing to reveal its owner. No matches in any database, no connections to known associates or suspects.

"How does someone leave that much DNA behind and not exist on record?" Damien asked, his voice tinged with disbelief.

"It's not impossible," Vincent replied. "If they've avoided hospitals, law enforcement, and any form of identification their whole life, they could slip through the cracks."

"It just doesn't make sense," Damien said, shaking his head. "Every step we take feels like someone's deliberately covering their tracks."

Vincent stared at the corkboard, his eyes fixated on the photographs of the victims. "It's more than that," he muttered. "This isn't just about covering tracks. This is someone playing a game."

Revisiting the Scene :

Desperate for clarity, Vincent and Damien returned to the Darlington mansion. The sprawling estate, once a symbol of power and opulence, now felt desolate and foreboding. They combed through the crime scenes again, retracing their steps, searching for anything they might have overlooked.

In Evelyn's bedroom, Vincent examined the faint remnants of the poison that had ended her life. "Sophisticated," he murmured. "Whoever did this knew what they were doing."

In the ballroom, Damien studied the chandelier rigged to kill Margaret. "It's precision work," he said. "This wasn't spur-of-the-moment."

Each murder scene echoed the same chilling message: the killer had planned meticulously. Yet, despite their methodical approach, they'd left behind a trail of clues that led nowhere.

The Interrogation Intensifies :

Frustration mounting, Vincent called Dalton, Charles, and Isabella back in for further questioning. This time, the gloves were off. The trio faced hours of relentless interrogation, each question designed to crack their defenses.

"Why did Augustus cut ties with you?" Vincent asked Charles, his voice sharp.

"Because I wouldn't bow to his demands," Charles replied, his tone defiant. "He wanted control over my life, my finances, everything. I walked away to protect my family."

"And yet, here you are," Vincent countered. "Why come back after all these years?"

Charles's jaw tightened. "Because despite everything, he was my brother. I came to pay my respects."

Vincent turned to Isabella. "What about you? Why were your hairs found in the hidden passage?"

"I told you," Isabella said firmly. "I stumbled upon it years ago, when we still visited the estate. It was a curiosity, nothing more."

Dalton, sitting silently, finally spoke up. "Detective, you're wasting your time. None of us did this. The real killer is out there, laughing at you."

Vincent's eyes narrowed. "If you're innocent, then prove it. Give me something to work with. Anything."

Dalton's silence was deafening.

The Growing Pressure :

As days turned into weeks, the pressure on Vincent intensified. The media's scrutiny grew harsher, painting him as a detective out of his depth. The government demanded progress.

"You need to take a break," Damien said one evening, finding Vincent hunched over his desk, a half-empty bottle of whiskey beside him.

"I don't have time for a break," Vincent snapped. "This case isn't just about solving a murder. It's about proving that no one—not even the untouchable Darlingsons—can escape justice."

Damien placed a hand on his shoulder. "You'll crack it, Vincent. You always do."

Vincent didn't respond, his mind already drifting back to the tangled web of clues and contradictions. He knew Damien's faith in him was steady, but his own confidence was waning. For the first time in his career, he wondered if the truth was truly within reach.

X

The Parcel of Shadows

Vincent Kane had always believed that persistence could break through any wall. Yet, the Darlington case was proving to be a fortress, its secrets hidden behind layers of cunning deception. He returned home late one night, weary from another fruitless day of chasing ghosts, only to find a small, nondescript parcel waiting for him on his doorstep. The sight of it sent a chill through his spine. No one knew his home address—not officially, at least.

He brought the package inside, placing it on the dining table. The weight of it felt oddly familiar. Carefully, he unwrapped it, his heart pounding with a mix of anticipation and dread. Inside was an object that made his breath hitch—a blood-stained knife, encased in a sealed plastic bag. Alongside it was a note, the handwriting erratic and unfamiliar:

"To uncover the truth, you must first face the shadows. - A Friend."

Vincent's hands trembled slightly as he studied the knife. It was no ordinary blade; it bore intricate engravings, the kind of craftsmanship reserved for collectors or assassins. Without wasting a moment, he called Damien.

"Damien, get to my house. Now. We've got a development."

The Weapon of Death :

When Damien arrived, Vincent handed him the parcel. "This is the murder weapon," he said, his voice firm. "It matches the description we got from the autopsy reports—sharp, single-edged, and capable of inflicting the precise wound that killed Augustus."

Damien examined the knife, nodding gravely. "The blood...it must be Augustus's. But why send it to you now? And who's this 'friend'?"

"Whoever sent this wants us to find something," Vincent replied. "But it's a taunt as much as it is a clue. They're playing with us."

Vincent immediately secured the knife and note in evidence bags and sent them to the forensic lab. The priority was clear: analyze the blood, test for fingerprints, and cross-match any DNA found.

The Cryptic Note :

Back at the office, Vincent pinned the note to his corkboard, its taunting message a stark reminder of how elusive the killer remained. Damien sat across from him, the tension palpable.

"What do you think they mean by 'face the shadows'?" Damien asked.

"It's symbolic," Vincent said, staring at the note. "The shadows could represent the hidden truths of the Darlington family or even my own failures in this case. Either way, it's meant to unnerve us."

"Do you think it's the killer who sent this?"

"Possibly," Vincent replied. "But it could also be someone close to the case—someone who knows more than they've let on."

The Breakthrough :

Two days later, the forensic lab delivered its report. The results sent a ripple of shock through Vincent and Damien.

"The blood on the knife is Augustus Darlington's," Damien read aloud, his voice steady. "And the fingerprints? They match the unidentified DNA profile we've been chasing."

Vincent leaned back in his chair, his mind racing. "So, the owner of that DNA not only touched the victims but also handled the murder weapon."

"And yet we still don't know who they are," Damien said bitterly. "No matches in any database. It's like they don't exist."

"They exist," Vincent said, his tone resolute. "They've just covered their tracks so well that we're left chasing shadows."

Revisiting the Case :

With this new evidence, Vincent and Damien poured over every detail of the case once more. They revisited old interviews, re-examined forensics, and scrutinized financial records. Yet, every lead seemed to spiral back into the same frustrating conclusion: the unidentified profile was the key, but without a match, they were stuck.

Vincent's frustration boiled over one night as he stared at the corkboard. "This person," he muttered, pointing to a blank silhouette representing the unknown suspect, "is laughing at us. They've orchestrated this entire thing, and we're dancing to their tune."

Damien, ever the voice of reason, said, "We're closer than we were yesterday, Vincent. The knife is proof they're not untouchable. They slipped up, and we'll catch them."

The Psychological Toll :

As days turned into nights, the case began to take a toll on Vincent. His once-steely resolve wavered, his confidence shaken. The cryptic note haunted him, its message replaying in his mind like a sinister mantra.

One evening, Damien found Vincent sitting alone in his office, the lights dimmed. "You need to rest," Damien said gently. "This case is eating you alive."

"I can't rest," Vincent replied, his voice hollow. "Not while they're out there. Not while the Darlington family's blood cries for justice."

Damien placed a reassuring hand on his shoulder. "We'll find them. Together."

A New Lead :

The next morning, a thought struck Vincent. He called Damien and said, "What if the note wasn't just a taunt? What if it's pointing us to something we've missed?"

"Like what?" Damien asked.

"I don't know yet," Vincent admitted. "But we need to dig deeper into the Darlington family's past. There's something there—something in the shadows—that we haven't uncovered."

As they prepared to dive back into the case with renewed determination, one thing was clear: the killer had made their move. It was now up to Vincent and Damien to make theirs.

This captures the escalating tension and frustration of the investigation while introducing a critical piece of evidence that brings them closer to the truth.

XI

The Missing Documents

Vincent Kane's office was a battlefield, papers strewn about like casualties of his relentless pursuit of justice. He had barely slept since the parcel's arrival. His mind raced with possibilities, but no answers came. A knock at the door startled him from his thoughts. Damien entered, holding his phone.

"Vincent, the family lawyer called," Damien said. "He's found something—important information about the Darlington family's history. He says it could be a breakthrough."

For the first time in days, Vincent's eyes brightened. "Finally, some progress. Tell him to come to my office immediately."

As Damien relayed the message, Vincent leaned back in his chair. A glimmer of hope pierced the darkness that had shrouded the case.

The Unexpected Call :

While they waited for the lawyer, Damien's phone buzzed again. He answered, his brow furrowing as he listened. "It's the forensic lab," he said, turning to Vincent. "The criminal psychologist wants to discuss something urgent."

Vincent hesitated. "You go," he said finally. "I'll stay here and meet the lawyer. If he's found something crucial, we need to act on it immediately."

Damien nodded and left. Vincent returned to his desk, his thoughts oscillating between the parcel, the lawyer's findings, and the elusive killer. Minutes stretched into an hour, then another. The lawyer had yet to arrive.

The Tragedy Deepens :

Just as Vincent was about to call Damien, his phone buzzed. The voice on the other end was urgent and grim. "Detective Kane, this is Officer Brown. We've got a situation. The Darlington family's lawyer, Mr. James, has been shot dead in his home."

Vincent's blood ran cold. "What?" he said, barely above a whisper. "When?"

"An hour ago," the officer replied. "His neighbors reported hearing gunshots. When we arrived, we found him in his study. The place was ransacked, and any documents he might have had are missing."

Vincent slammed his fist on the desk. "Secure the scene. I'll be there shortly."

The Crime Scene :

When Vincent arrived at the lawyer's home, it was chaos. Officers cordoned off the area, reporters swarmed outside, and forensic teams combed through the study. Vincent pushed past them, his jaw set in anger and frustration.

The study was a mess. Books and papers littered the floor, drawers were yanked out, and the strongbox in the corner lay open and empty. Mr. James's body slumped over the desk, a bullet wound in his chest.

"What do we have?" Vincent asked the lead investigator.

"Single gunshot wound, point-blank range," the investigator replied. "No signs of forced entry. Whoever did this knew what they were looking for."

Vincent's eyes scanned the room, taking in every detail. "What about security footage? Neighbors? Witnesses?"

"We're checking," the investigator said. "But so far, no leads."

Vincent's frustration boiled over. He turned to Damien, who had just arrived. "They're always one step ahead. Whoever this is, they're playing a game, and we're losing."

The Missing Link :

Back at the office, Vincent paced the floor, his mind racing. The lawyer's death was no coincidence. Whoever killed him wanted to erase whatever he had uncovered. But what was so damning that it warranted murder?

Damien watched him silently for a moment before speaking. "Vincent, we'll find them. They've made a mistake. Sending that parcel, killing the lawyer—it's reckless. They're getting desperate."

"Or they're trying to mislead us," Vincent said bitterly. "We need to figure out what Mr. James found. Start by tracing his last phone calls, emails, anything."

The Breakthrough That Never Was :

As they dug into the lawyer's communications, a pattern began to emerge. Mr. James had been in contact with several people linked to the Darlington family, including Augustus's estranged brother and sister-in-law. He had also accessed bank records, property deeds, and old court filings.

But the trail ended abruptly.

"It's like he knew he was onto something," Damien said. "But he didn't have time to finish."

Vincent stared at the corkboard, now overflowing with threads of the case. The cryptic note, the parcel, the knife, the unidentified DNA—it all pointed to a shadowy figure manipulating events from the periphery.

"This isn't just about money or power," Vincent said quietly. "It's personal. Whoever did this has a vendetta against the Darlington family."

A Fractured Resolve :

The weight of the case bore down on Vincent. Every lead seemed to end in more questions. The killer's audacity—sending the murder weapon, killing the lawyer—was a constant reminder of how far they were willing to go.

Damien broke the silence. "What now?"

Vincent sighed, rubbing his temples. "We keep digging. The answers are there. We just have to find them."

But as the night stretched on, Vincent couldn't shake the feeling that the killer was watching, waiting for their next move. The shadows seemed to grow darker, the stakes higher. And for the first time in his career, Vincent Kane doubted if he would ever find the light.

XII

A Dead End

Vincent Kane's office was shrouded in a tense silence as the latest twist in the Darlington case unfolded. The killer of the family lawyer, Mr. James, had been found dead in an abandoned warehouse on the outskirts of the city. The body was discovered by a maintenance worker, sprawled on the cold concrete floor, riddled with gunshot wounds. No murder weapon was recovered, and there were no witnesses.

For Vincent, the discovery raised more questions than answers. The chain of death seemed endless, and every lead turned into a dead end. As he stood over the latest victim's body at the crime scene, his frustration grew. The killer's identity remained a mystery, their motives shrouded in an impenetrable fog.

The crime scene itself offered little in terms of evidence. The forensics team scoured the area but found no DNA traces other than the victim's. The lack of surveillance footage and witnesses made it clear this murder was a professional hit.

A City on Edge :

Back at his office, Vincent stared at the photographs pinned to his corkboard. Each face stared back at him: Augustus, Evelyn, Henry, Margaret, Victor, Ophelia, Samantha, Mr. James—and now the lawyer's murderer. The board was a tangled mess of red strings and annotations, yet none of it pointed to a definitive answer.

Damien entered, a stack of reports in hand. "The autopsy's in. The shooter was precise—two shots to the chest, one to the head. Execution style. Whoever did this wanted to send a message."

"To whom?" Vincent asked, exasperated. "The Darlington family is gone. The lawyer's dead. Now their killer is dead too. It's like we're chasing ghosts."

"Maybe that's the point," Damien said. "Whoever is behind this wants to keep us in the dark."

Helplessness Sets In :

Vincent had been in difficult situations before, but this case was testing his limits. Days turned into sleepless nights as he poured over documents, revisited old crime scenes, and interrogated anyone even remotely connected to the Darlington family. Yet, every effort seemed futile. Clues led to dead ends, and suspects either ended up dead or exonerated. The case was unraveling faster than he could piece it together.

One evening, Vincent found himself sitting alone in his dimly lit office, his head in his hands. The weight of the investigation pressed heavily on his shoulders. For the first time in his career, he felt truly helpless.

"What am I missing?" he muttered to himself. "What piece of the puzzle hasn't been uncovered?"

A Desperate Move :

Desperation led Vincent to revisit every shred of evidence, no matter how insignificant it seemed. He ordered Damien to recheck the DNA results, the financial records, and even the cryptic note that had accompanied the murder weapon. He requested surveillance footage from miles around the lawyer's residence, though he knew it was a long shot.

Damien's voice broke through Vincent's thoughts. "We've hit every lead, Vincent. Every angle. Maybe it's time to bring in outside help."

"No," Vincent snapped. "This is my case. My responsibility."

"But you're running yourself into the ground," Damien said gently. "This isn't just about solving the case anymore. It's about proving something to yourself."

Vincent didn't respond. He couldn't. Damien was right, but admitting it felt like surrendering to the chaos.

An Empty Trail:

The days that followed were marked by relentless yet fruitless effort. Vincent tracked down old acquaintances of the Darlington family, hoping to uncover a motive buried in the past. He revisited the mansion, walking through its silent, ominous halls, searching for something—anything—that might have been overlooked.

Despite his best efforts, the case seemed to resist resolution. The unidentified DNA profile remained an enigma. The motives behind the murders were elusive, and the trail of the true mastermind had gone cold. Even the parcel with the murder weapon, which Vincent initially thought would be a breakthrough, had led nowhere.

The pressure mounted as media outlets began to criticize the investigation. Headlines like "Detective Kane: Genius or Failure?" and "Darlington Case in Limbo" only added to his burden. The world was watching, and Vincent felt the weight of their judgment.

Breaking Point :

Late one night, Vincent sat in his office, the glow of his desk lamp illuminating the files scattered before him. He picked up the photograph of Augustus Darlington and stared into the eyes of the man whose death had sparked this cascade of tragedy.

"What were you hiding, Augustus?" he whispered. "What's the secret worth killing for?"

His phone buzzed, pulling him from his thoughts. It was Damien.

"Vincent, you need to go home. You've been at this for days."

"I can't stop now," Vincent replied, his voice weary. "If I stop, I might miss something."

"Or you might collapse," Damien countered. "This case isn't going anywhere tonight. Get some rest."

Reluctantly, Vincent agreed. As he drove home through the empty streets, he couldn't shake the feeling that the case was slipping further from his grasp. For the first time, he began to doubt himself.

A Glimmer of Hope :

The next morning, Vincent awoke with a renewed sense of determination. He arrived at the office early, hoping that fresh eyes and a clear mind might reveal something he had missed. But as he sifted through the evidence once more, the same frustrating patterns emerged.

The Darlington case had become a labyrinth, and Vincent was trapped at its center. Yet, despite his mounting frustration, he knew one thing for certain: he couldn't give up. Somewhere in the shadows, the truth was waiting to be found.

XIII

Clues in Shadows

Vincent Kane's relentless pursuit of the truth often felt like chasing the wind, and the latest developments in the Darlington case were no exception. Days of exhaustive investigation had yielded what appeared to be a breakthrough: five new clues had surfaced. Yet, each one seemed as elusive as the shadows that haunted Vincent's thoughts.

The Five Clues :

The first lead came in the form of a phone call. A witness had reported seeing a black sedan parked outside the Darlington estate on the night of the murders. The second clue emerged from a long-overlooked financial transaction—a sizable transfer from one of Augustus Darlington's offshore accounts to an unknown recipient days before his death. The third clue was a torn piece of fabric discovered near the hidden passage where Damien had found the long hairs earlier. Forensic analysis suggested it belonged to a high-end coat.

The fourth lead was more cryptic: an anonymous tip sent via email claimed that the Darlington family had a "hidden ledger" detailing their darkest secrets. The email, however, was routed through multiple servers, making its origin nearly impossible to trace. The fifth and final clue was perhaps the most baffling. A set of coordinates had been scribbled on a scrap of paper found in the lawyer's belongings, leading to a remote, abandoned building on the city's outskirts.

Vincent and Damien wasted no time following up on these clues, but each one seemed to dissolve under scrutiny.

The Vanishing Sedan :

Damien tracked down traffic surveillance footage from the night in question, focusing on the black sedan. Yet, despite hours of footage review, the vehicle's plates were unreadable, and its movements erratic. The car seemed to vanish into thin air, leaving behind nothing but questions.

"Could it have been a rental?" Damien wondered aloud as he and Vincent reviewed the footage.

"Possibly," Vincent replied, his voice edged with frustration. "But without a plate number, it's like looking for a needle in a haystack."

The Offshore Mystery :

The financial transaction proved equally vexing. The offshore account was registered in Augustus's name, but the recipient was listed as "The Benevolent Trust," a shell company with no known address or owners. Attempts to trace the trust led to dead ends, as the trail disappeared into a labyrinth of fake identities and proxy accounts.

"It's like they knew we'd find this," Vincent muttered. "They covered their tracks too well."

Damien nodded. "Whoever orchestrated this knew exactly what they were doing. This wasn't some spur-of-the-moment act."

The Fabric and the Ledger :

The torn piece of fabric was sent to the lab, but the results were inconclusive. The material was custom-made, sold exclusively to high-end clientele. Attempts to trace its origin yielded a list of buyers, none of whom had any apparent connection to the Darlington family.

The hidden ledger mentioned in the email was even more elusive. Despite scouring the Darlington estate and interviewing surviving acquaintances, no one could confirm its existence. If such a document existed, it was hidden far too well.

The Abandoned Coordinates :

The final clue—the coordinates—led to an eerie, decaying warehouse on the outskirts of the city. Vincent and Damien searched the premises thoroughly, but all they found were remnants of squatters and graffiti-covered walls. There was no evidence linking the site to the Darlington case.

"It's like someone is playing a game with us," Damien said as they left the building. "Dangling clues just out of reach."

Vincent's Revelation :

By the end of the week, the mounting dead ends took their toll on Vincent. He sat alone in his office, the corkboard filled with photographs, documents, and red string now resembling a chaotic web of futility. Each clue had seemed promising, yet none had led to the answers he desperately sought.

Damien entered, a weary look on his face. "Anything new?"

Vincent shook his head. "Nothing. We're running in circles."

Damien sat across from him, silence stretching between them. Finally, he said, "Maybe we're looking too hard.

Maybe the answer isn't in the clues."

"What do you mean?" Vincent asked, leaning forward.

"I mean...what if the killer is closer than we think? Someone who knows how we operate. Someone who knows how to mislead us."

The thought lingered in the air, heavy with implication. Vincent leaned back in his chair, his mind racing. Could Damien be right? Could the killer be someone within their circle, watching their every move?

Vincent stood abruptly, his eyes narrowing with determination. "If that's true, then they've been underestimating us. We need to rethink our approach."

"And what's the plan?" Damien asked.

Vincent glanced at the corkboard, then back at Damien. "We stop chasing shadows and start watching the people closest to us. The killer isn't running from us—they're hiding in plain sight."

XIV

Shadows Watching Shadows.

With Vincent Kane's realization that the killer might be hiding in plain sight, the investigation took a sharp turn. He ordered Damien to assemble a list of every individual associated with the Darlington family—friends, employees, distant relatives, even casual acquaintances. It was time to scrutinize every connection with a fresh set of eyes.

A Web of Observation :

Vincent and Damien divided the names between them, assigning each one a dedicated observer from their trusted team. Bank accounts, phone records, travel logs—nothing was off-limits. They began to shadow suspects discreetly, keeping their surveillance airtight and their movements untraceable.

One particular individual caught their attention early: Nathaniel, the Darlington family's long-time butler. His loyalty to Augustus was well-documented, but his stoic demeanor and evasive responses during previous interrogations had raised flags. Another focus was Patricia Hargrove, Evelyn's best friend, who had mysteriously flown to Paris days after the murders. Her sudden departure seemed suspicious, though she claimed it was a pre-planned trip.

A Family's Hidden Past :

Amid their investigations, Damien unearthed something peculiar: a decades-old lawsuit involving the Darlington family and a business partner who had accused Augustus's father of fraud. The case had been settled out of court, but not before the Darlington name was dragged through the mud. The plaintiff, Edgar Watts, had disappeared shortly after the settlement, leaving behind a trail of financial ruin.

Could this old grudge have festered over the years, turning into a motive for revenge?

"We need to track down Edgar's family," Vincent decided. "If he's dead, someone might still be nursing his resentment."

A Strange Discovery :

As Vincent and Damien sifted through these tangled connections, another peculiar thread emerged. While reviewing Augustus's financial records, they found a string of transactions labeled only as "Donations." These were not to charities but to a single, untraceable account. The amounts varied, but they occurred monthly for nearly two years leading up to the murders.

"Blackmail?" Damien suggested, setting down the papers.

"Possibly," Vincent replied, his mind racing. "Or hush money. Either way, someone was benefiting."

Tracing the account led to a dead end—the funds were withdrawn in cash almost immediately after each deposit.

Still, it was another piece of the puzzle.

A Cryptic Note's Return :

Just as Vincent was beginning to feel that their efforts were yielding some progress, a package arrived at his home. It was wrapped in plain brown paper, its edges meticulously folded. Inside was another cryptic note, scrawled in the same jagged handwriting as the one accompanying the murder weapon.

"The truth hides where the past bleeds. Will you have the courage to face it?"

The ominous message sent a chill down Vincent's spine. He immediately sent the note to the forensics lab for analysis, focusing on handwriting comparison. A day later, the results confirmed his fears: the handwriting matched that of the previous note.

"Whoever this is, they're watching us," Damien said, his tone grim. "They know exactly what we're doing."

The Shadow's Influence :

Vincent couldn't shake the feeling that the killer was toying with him. The notes weren't just clues; they were psychological warfare. Every time Vincent felt he was gaining ground, the killer pulled him back into uncertainty. It was as though they enjoyed watching him struggle.

The note's reference to the past resonated with him. What about the Darlington family's history had he overlooked? The lawyer's murder—and the theft of the documents he'd uncovered—hinted at something damning, something worth killing for.

Observing the Observers :

As days turned into a week, Vincent's team reported little progress. Nathaniel's routines were maddeningly ordinary. Patricia's Paris trip was genuine; she'd attended a fashion conference with verifiable records. Edgar Watts's family, meanwhile, seemed to have no ties to the Darlington case—though Vincent noted a lingering bitterness in his son's tone during their brief phone conversation.

But Vincent's instincts told him to dig deeper. He began to suspect that their efforts were being deliberately thwarted.

"What if the killer isn't just watching us?" he proposed one evening. "What if they're among us?"

Damien's expression darkened. "You think we have a mole?"

"I think it's possible," Vincent admitted. "We're not dealing with a common murderer. This person is intelligent, calculated, and always one step ahead."

Unraveling the Past :

Vincent turned his attention to the Darlington archives stored in the city's legal records office. He spent hours poring over contracts, lawsuits, and personal correspondence. It was there, buried in a decades-old letter, that he found a potential lead: a reference to a "sealed agreement" between Augustus and an unnamed third party. The agreement's contents were not disclosed, but the language suggested something scandalous.

"This might be it," Vincent murmured. He tasked Damien with obtaining a court order to unseal the document, hoping it would provide the breakthrough they needed.

A Killer's Confidence :

As the days passed, Vincent couldn't ignore the growing sense of dread. The killer was bold enough to deliver notes to his home, confident enough to leave cryptic messages that seemed designed to taunt him. Yet, they remained elusive, their identity hidden behind layers of misdirection.

The truth was close, Vincent could feel it. But the closer he got, the more dangerous the game became.

XV

Buried Secrets Unravels

Vincent Kane sat in his office, his fingers laced tightly together as he stared at the corkboard in front of him. The photographs, notes, and diagrams pinned to it formed a chaotic web that mirrored his mental state. He had been chasing shadows for weeks, and every step forward seemed to push him two steps back. The stolen documents, the cryptic notes, the unrelenting sense of someone manipulating the investigation from behind the scenes—it was all beginning to wear on him.

Damien Frost burst into the office, visibly out of breath, holding a set of blueprints and a collection of envelopes. "Vincent, you're not going to believe this," he said, placing the items on the desk.

"What now?" Vincent asked, his tone carrying more fatigue than curiosity.

Damien slid a torn envelope across the desk. "The seal on the Darlington documents... it was broken before we could arrange to open it officially. The entire collection is gone."

Vincent's eyes flared with fury. "What do you mean, gone?" He grabbed the envelope, inspecting it for any sign of tampering.

"I mean stolen," Damien clarified. "We secured the vault and left the documents untouched until we could bring in the proper authorities. When I returned this morning, the vault was wide open. Whoever did this knew exactly what they were looking for."

Vincent slammed his fist on the desk. "That was our one lead. Everything pointed to those documents containing something crucial. Damn it, Damien, how could this happen under our watch?"

Damien shook his head, his expression clouded with guilt. "There were no signs of forced entry. The culprit had access—either someone within the investigation or someone with connections to the Darlington estate."

Vincent pushed his chair back and stood, pacing the room. "This isn't just about solving the murders anymore. This... this is someone toying with us. They're always one step ahead, and they're enjoying it."

A tense silence hung between them before Damien spoke again. "There's more. The forensics team re-examined the cryptic notes. It's confirmed: both were written by the same person. Whoever this is, they're intentionally engaging with you, Vincent. It's personal."

Vincent sat back down, his mind racing. "Who has access to this level of information? Who would benefit from orchestrating this chaos? It has to be someone who knows the Darlington family inside out."

Damien hesitated, then placed another folder on the desk. "I... I've been looking into Augustus Darlington's inner circle. Close associates, former employees, estranged relatives. There's something strange about their connections—patterns that don't add up."

Vincent opened the folder and scanned the documents. The names were familiar—relatives, business partners, even loyal staff—but the details were peculiar. Bank transactions with unusual timestamps, overlapping alibis that seemed too convenient, and unexplained communications between people who were supposedly estranged.

"You think the culprit is someone from this list?" Vincent asked.

Damien nodded. "It's a possibility. We need to start tailing these individuals, observing their movements. If one of them is the mastermind, they'll slip up eventually."

Over the next few days, the team mobilized. Surveillance was set up on all potential suspects, and Damien led a smaller team to re-examine every inch of the Darlington estate, hoping to uncover something—anything—that had been missed before. Vincent, meanwhile, poured over the stolen documents' inventory, reconstructing what might have been taken and why.

"It's a frustrating cycle," Vincent muttered to himself late one evening, staring at a map of the estate. "Every time we get close, the ground shifts beneath us."

Just as he was about to call it a night, his phone buzzed. It was Damien.

"Vincent, we found something odd in the estate's west wing. A hidden alcove behind one of the bookcases. It looks like someone had been using it recently."

"What did you find?" Vincent asked, his heart quickening.

"A single key, unmarked, and a stack of correspondence addressed to... Augustus's brother. We're sending it to the lab for prints and analysis."

Vincent's mind raced. Why would Augustus's brother have secret correspondence hidden within the estate? Could it be connected to the stolen documents? The mystery deepened with every discovery, yet the answers remained elusive.

The next morning, a courier arrived at Vincent's residence with another package. This one contained no weapon but rather an ornate Darlington family heirloom—a pocket watch engraved with cryptic initials. A note accompanied it:

Time reveals all truths, Mr. Kane. Are you running out of it?

Vincent stared at the watch, its ticking unnervingly loud in the quiet room. Whoever this was, they were taunting him, reminding him that he was being watched.

When he brought the pocket watch to the lab, the results were once again maddening. The fingerprints were smudged beyond recognition, and the engraving provided no immediate clues.

Damien's frustration mirrored Vincent's as they met at the office later that day. "It's like they're daring us to catch them," Damien said, throwing his hands up in exasperation.

Vincent leaned back in his chair, the weight of the case pressing down on him. "No, it's worse. They're playing us, Damien. Every clue, every lead, it's all part of their game. And the longer we're caught in it, the more control they have."

Damien's phone buzzed, interrupting their conversation. He read the message and looked up, his face grim. "The lab's done analyzing the correspondence. There's something you need to see."

Vincent grabbed his coat. "Let's go."

The lab report was a mixed bag of frustration and intrigue. The correspondence contained veiled threats, cryptic references to financial disputes, and mentions of a "hidden truth" that could ruin the Darlington family. But the most chilling revelation was a single phrase repeated in several letters:

The sins of the father shall be visited upon the children.

Vincent stared at the phrase, his mind churning. "They're not just after revenge. This is about legacy. Whoever this is, they want to destroy the Darlington name, root and branch."

Damien nodded, his expression grim. "And they're doing a damn good job of it."

As Vincent and Damien left the lab that night, the weight of the case pressed heavily on their shoulders. The killer was close—of that, Vincent was certain. But whether they could uncover the truth before the Darlington family's legacy was completely obliterated remained a question without an answer.

XVI

The Ties That Bind

The discovery of the black sedan traced back to Kyle Richardson's extended family set off a whirlwind of activity. For weeks, Vincent and Damien had pursued tenuous leads, dead-end clues, and cryptic notes that teased but never delivered clarity. This new development finally seemed like a tangible lead—something they could sink their teeth into.

The Interrogation Begins :

Kyle Richardson was summoned to the precinct immediately. His usual air of confidence seemed dimmed as he walked into the interrogation room, a far cry from the composed businessman he typically presented himself as. Vincent sat across the table, his gaze sharp and unrelenting.

"Kyle," Vincent began, his voice measured, "we've traced the black sedan to your family. Care to explain?"

Kyle shifted uncomfortably in his chair. "I—I don't know what you're talking about. I don't own a black sedan."

Damien leaned against the wall, arms crossed. "It's registered under one of your relatives. You sure you don't have any idea who might've been driving it the night

Augustus Darlington was murdered?"

Kyle hesitated, beads of sweat forming on his forehead. "I... I can't say for sure. My cousin Max owns a black sedan, but he lives three states away. I haven't seen him in months."

Vincent leaned forward, narrowing his eyes. "Convenient. But we're not talking about months ago; we're talking about the night of the murders. You're telling me you have no idea what someone in your own family might've been doing on that specific night?"

Kyle opened his mouth to respond, but his voice faltered. He looked trapped, his nervousness escalating with each passing second.

The Narco Test :

Given his evident anxiety, Vincent ordered another narco-analysis test for Kyle. The results would likely be inconclusive again, but Vincent was determined to leave no stone unturned. The procedure began under strict supervision, with psychologists and forensic experts present.

"What do you know about the black sedan?" the expert asked Kyle during the session.

Kyle, in a groggy state, mumbled, "I don't know... I don't know who was driving it."

"Were you involved in the Darlington murders?"

"No... I swear, no."

The experts noted Kyle's heart rate and demeanor. He appeared consistent, showing no signs of deception, yet his anxiety persisted.

"Who do you think might've been involved?"

Kyle's eyes fluttered. "I don't know... but someone close. Someone... dangerous."

Sheriff's Frustration Boils Over

The mounting tension reached a breaking point when the Sheriff stormed into Vincent's office later that day.

"Enough is enough, Vincent!" the Sheriff bellowed, slamming a stack of files onto the desk. "This case is turning into a circus. Do you have any idea how much pressure I'm under from the feds, the media, and the damn government? And here you are, chasing shadows!"

Vincent glared at the Sheriff, his jaw tightening. "You think I don't know the stakes? I've been working around the clock, piecing together this mess. But if you want to pull the plug, go ahead. Let's see someone else handle this disaster."

"This isn't just about you, Vincent," the Sheriff retorted. "It's about results. And right now, you're not delivering."

Damien stepped in, his voice calm but firm. "Sheriff, we're closer than ever. We've identified the car, we're narrowing down the suspects, and the notes—"

"The notes are a joke!" the Sheriff snapped. "Cryptic nonsense leading nowhere."

Vincent stood, his voice cold. "Then why don't you solve it, Sheriff? If it's so easy, take over."

The room fell into an uneasy silence. The Sheriff stormed out, leaving Vincent and Damien to stew in the tension.

A Glimmer of Insight :

That evening, Vincent pored over the case files in his dimly lit office. Damien sat across from him, flipping through the latest forensic reports.

"You think Kyle's hiding something?" Damien asked.

"Maybe. But if he is, he's damn good at it," Vincent muttered. "I don't trust him, though. He knows more than he's letting on."

"What about the black sedan? Should we bring his cousin Max in?"

Vincent nodded. "Do it. I want him here by tomorrow."

As they worked late into the night, Vincent couldn't shake the feeling that the killer was playing a game—a meticulous, calculated game that kept them perpetually one step behind.

The Burden of Doubt :

The weight of the case pressed heavily on Vincent's shoulders. He hadn't slept properly in days, and the constant dead ends were beginning to wear on him. He stared at the wall of evidence, the photographs and notes mocking him with their lack of cohesion.

"This case isn't about the Darlington fortune," Vincent said aloud, more to himself than to Damien.

Damien looked up, surprised. "What do you mean?"

"It's personal. The killer isn't just tying up loose ends or eliminating witnesses. They're taunting us. Leaving breadcrumbs to keep us chasing our tails."

Damien frowned. "If that's true, then they're close. Watching us."

Vincent's eyes darkened. "Exactly. And that's what terrifies me."

The Case Deepens :

Despite the frustration, Vincent refused to give up. The black sedan, the cryptic notes, the dead lawyer—it was all connected. He just needed to find the missing piece.

As the night wore on, Vincent leaned back in his chair, exhaustion evident in his posture. "Damien, call it a night. We'll pick this up tomorrow."

Damien hesitated but eventually nodded, leaving Vincent alone in the office. The detective sat in silence, the weight of the unsolved murders pressing down on him like a physical burden.

Somewhere, the killer was out there, watching, waiting, and laughing at their efforts. Vincent clenched his fists. He wouldn't let them win.

XVII

The Innocence of Max Richardson

Max Richardson was brought into the station the next morning. Unlike his cousin Kyle, Max carried himself with a certain calmness, a quiet demeanor that made it difficult to gauge his guilt or innocence. He didn't seem rattled by the accusations or the evidence linking his car to the Darlington estate the night of Augustus's murder.

Vincent Kane and Damien Frost sat across from Max in the interrogation room, their expressions unreadable.

"Max," Vincent began, leaning forward, "your black sedan was seen near the Darlington mansion on the night Augustus Darlington was murdered. Care to explain?"

Max tilted his head slightly, his brow furrowed in confusion. "I think you've got the wrong man, Detective. My car's been parked in my garage for weeks. I haven't even driven it."

Vincent smirked, but there was no humor in his eyes. "Do you expect me to believe that someone just borrowed your car without your knowledge and used it to commit a murder?"

Max crossed his arms, his voice steady. "That's exactly what I'm saying. I live in a gated community. My garage is locked, but it's not impossible to break into. If someone wanted to use my car, they could've done it without me knowing."

The Long Interrogation :

For hours, Vincent and Damien peppered Max with questions, circling back to the same points, probing for inconsistencies.

"Where were you on the night of the murder?" Damien asked.

"I was home, watching TV. Alone," Max replied.

"No alibi, then?" Vincent pressed.

Max shrugged. "No one to back me up, if that's what you mean. But I didn't leave my house."

"Do you have any connection to the Darlington family?"

"Only through Kyle," Max said. "I've met Augustus a few times at business functions, but I wouldn't say I knew him personally."

"And you expect us to believe you had no reason to be at the mansion that night?"

"That's exactly what I'm saying," Max said firmly.

Damien's Observations :

As the hours dragged on, Damien began to notice something peculiar about Max: he didn't exhibit the typical signs of a guilty man. There was no evasiveness, no hesitation in his answers. He seemed almost too cooperative, which made Damien wonder if they were barking up the wrong tree.

When Vincent stepped out to review the evidence with the forensic team, Damien decided to take a different approach.

"Max, you seem pretty calm for someone accused of being connected to a murder," Damien said.

Max sighed. "Because I know I didn't do it. Look, Detective, I get why you're questioning me. The car's registered in my name, and that's suspicious. But I don't know how else to prove that I wasn't involved."

"Do you think Kyle could've used your car?" Damien asked.

Max hesitated for the first time. "Kyle and I aren't close, but... he's not the type to get his hands dirty. If anything, he'd hire someone to do his dirty work."

Forensic Evidence Review:

Vincent returned with a file in hand, his expression grim. "Max, we ran forensic tests on your car. There are no prints, no DNA, nothing to suggest you've even been in it recently. Care to explain?"

Max exhaled deeply, relief evident in his eyes. "Because I haven't been in it recently. Like I said, someone must've taken it."

"What about the GPS logs?" Damien asked Vincent.

"The GPS was disabled the night of the murder," Vincent said. "Whoever took the car knew what they were doing."

"See?" Max said. "I'm telling the truth. Whoever used my car is the one you're looking for."

Max's Alibi Confirmed:

Despite the lack of concrete evidence against Max, Vincent wasn't ready to let him off the hook just yet. He ordered a thorough review of Max's phone records, security footage from his neighborhood, and any other information that could corroborate his story.

A day later, the results came in: Max's phone had been pinging from his home the entire night of the murder.

Security footage from his gated community showed no sign of him leaving.

Vincent reluctantly admitted defeat. "It looks like you're in the clear, Max. For now."

Max stood, straightening his jacket. "I appreciate your diligence, Detective. But I hope you find the real killer soon. Whoever they are, they're a lot closer to you than you think."

Vincent's Frustration Mounts :

As Max walked out of the station, Vincent slammed his fist on the table. "Another dead end," he muttered.

Damien placed a hand on his shoulder. "We'll figure this out, Vincent. We always do."

Vincent shook his head. "We're running out of suspects, Damien. Every lead turns to ash in our hands. The killer is mocking us, staying one step ahead. And now, we've wasted precious time chasing shadows."

Damien tried to stay optimistic. "At least we've ruled out another suspect. That's progress."

Vincent didn't respond, his mind already racing with the next steps. Somewhere, the killer was watching, waiting, and laughing at their struggles

XVIII

The Forgotten Diary

The rain poured relentlessly as Vincent Kane approached the late lawyer's house under the cover of night. Armed with little more than his instincts, he was determined to unearth something—anything—that might give him the breakthrough he desperately needed. The case was slipping through his fingers, and the weight of failure gnawed at him.

The house, still sealed by police tape, loomed ominously in the darkness. Vincent slipped inside, his flashlight slicing through the gloom. The air inside was thick, filled with the faint scent of dust and despair. Papers were scattered across the floor from the prior investigation, and shattered glass crunched beneath his boots as he moved through the rooms.

Searching for a Hidden Truth:

Vincent began in the study, meticulously scanning shelves, drawers, and cabinets for anything that might have been overlooked. The lawyer had been an organized man, but chaos had taken over in his final hours. As Vincent sifted through piles of documents, he noticed a faint scratch along the baseboard near a tall bookshelf.

Something felt off.

He crouched down, running his fingers along the edge of the board. With a sharp tug, he dislodged a hidden panel, revealing a slim leather-bound diary tucked inside. The leather was worn, its edges frayed, as though it had been opened and closed countless times over the years.

Vincent's heart quickened as he flipped it open.

The Story Unfolds :

The handwriting was neat, deliberate, and dated back several decades. The first few pages were filled with mundane notes about legal cases and business dealings. But as Vincent turned the pages, the tone shifted dramatically.

It was the story of a family—a father, mother, and their young son. The father was a prominent businessman, deeply entangled in ventures with Augustus Darlington. According to the diary, the partnership had been amicable at first, but cracks began to form as Augustus's ambition grew.

One fateful night, the diary recounted, the two men were sharing whiskey and discussing a significant investment opportunity. An argument erupted, fueled by both alcohol and greed. The father, unwilling to compromise, stormed out of Augustus's mansion.

But Augustus, blinded by rage and a desire to protect his interests, followed him. On a desolate stretch of road, Augustus confronted his business partner, and in a fit of fury, killed him.

The Cover-Up :

The diary described how Augustus, wielding his immense influence, staged the scene to look like a tragic accident. The authorities, in awe of his power and wealth, dared not question him.

The man's widow, a gentle and reserved woman with no interest in business, became the next victim of Augustus's schemes. He manipulated her, offering a meager share of the business to placate her while seizing the lion's share of the assets.

But grief consumed her. The diary detailed how, unable to cope with the loss of her husband and the betrayal of someone she had trusted, the widow took her own life, leaving behind their young son.

A Helpless Boy

The son, left orphaned and alone, grew up in the shadow of Augustus's betrayal. The diary described him as a bright but sorrowful child, marked by the injustice that had stolen his family from him. He received no help, no compassion. Augustus ensured that any whispers of the truth were silenced, and the boy faded into obscurity.

As Vincent read the final lines of the entry, he felt a chill run down his spine. The diary ended abruptly, with no indication of who had written it or why it had been hidden in the lawyer's house.

A Shocking Revelation :

Closing the diary, Vincent sat back on his heels, his mind racing. If this story were true, it painted Augustus Darlington in a damning light, revealing a side of him that had been carefully hidden behind his empire's gilded façade. But more importantly, it introduced a new layer of mystery to the case.

Was the son still alive? Could he be the unidentified figure whose DNA had haunted the investigation?

Vincent stared at the diary, the rain outside echoing the storm within his mind. The case was no longer just about the Darlington murders—it was about decades of secrets, lies, and the devastating ripple effects of Augustus Darlington's greed and ambition.

He slipped the diary into his coat and left the house, his thoughts consumed by the tragic story of the family that Augustus had destroyed.

XIX

The Blade of
Betrayal

The rain was unrelenting as Vincent Kane stepped out of the late lawyer's house, the diary tucked securely in his coat. His thoughts swirled with the weight of the discovery—a decades-old tragedy buried under layers of lies and power. He had found a breakthrough, something that could finally unravel the case.

As Vincent walked down the driveway toward his car, headlights pierced the darkness. A sleek black sedan rolled to a stop, its wipers frantically swiping away the downpour. Vincent's hand instinctively moved to his coat pocket, where his gun rested.

The door of the sedan opened, and out stepped Damien Frost.

A Familiar Face in the Storm :

"Damien!" Vincent called out, relief flooding his voice. The sight of his trusted ally brought a rare sense of comfort. "What are you doing here? I didn't think I'd see you tonight."

Damien, his face shrouded in shadows, stepped closer. He was drenched from the rain, his usual composure replaced by a strange, almost haunted expression.

Vincent rushed to him, his face alight with excitement. "You won't believe what I've found. This is the break we've been waiting for. The diary—it's all here. The whole story about Augustus and—"

Before Vincent could finish, Damien embraced him tightly. The hug caught Vincent off guard, but he returned it, clapping Damien on the back.

"Damien, we've got him," Vincent said, his voice filled with hope.

The Betrayal :

Then Vincent felt it—a sharp, searing pain in his back. His body stiffened as the realization hit him.

Damien had stabbed him.

The shock rendered Vincent speechless. He staggered backward, clutching at the hilt of the knife now embedded in his back. His eyes locked onto Damien's, searching for an explanation, a reason.

"Damien," he gasped, his voice barely a whisper. "Why?"

Damien's face was a mixture of anguish and resolve. "I'm sorry, Vincent," he said, his voice trembling. "I didn't want it to come to this. But you were never supposed to find out. The boy... his name was Damien Frost."

The words hit Vincent harder than the blade. His trusted partner, his closest ally, was the boy from the diary—the son of the man Augustus had killed all those years ago.

The Truth Revealed :

Vincent stumbled, the pain and betrayal overwhelming him. Damien caught him briefly, lowering him to the ground as rain mixed with the blood seeping from Vincent's wound.

"I didn't want you to be part of this," Damien said, his voice breaking. "You were the only one who ever believed in me, who ever treated me like more than just another tool. But Augustus destroyed my family, and I swore I'd make them all pay. Every single one of them."

Vincent tried to speak, but his voice failed him. His mind raced, piecing together the fragments of the story. Damien had been orchestrating everything—the murders, the notes, the misdirection. All of it had been part of his plan for revenge.

"I never wanted to hurt you," Damien continued, his eyes glistening with tears. "But you got too close. I couldn't let you stop me. Not now."

Falling into Darkness :

Vincent's vision blurred as the blood loss and shock took hold. His grip on the diary loosened, and it slipped from his hand, landing in the mud.

Damien picked it up, his face a mask of sorrow and determination. "I'll finish this, Vincent. I promise you that."

With that, Damien climbed back into the black sedan and drove away, leaving Vincent lying in the rain, his body growing cold.

As the darkness closed in, Vincent's thoughts were a chaotic mix of pain, betrayal, and determination. He couldn't let it end like this. Not without stopping Damien. Not without uncovering the truth.

The last thing he saw before losing consciousness was the glow of distant headlights approaching—the faint promise of salvation.

XX

Awakening to Shadows

The hum of machines and the antiseptic scent of the hospital room pulled Vincent Kane out of the murky depths of unconsciousness. His body felt heavy, every breath a laborious effort, as though the weight of the betrayal he had suffered pressed down on his chest. Blinking against the sterile white light, he turned his head slowly.

A familiar figure sat by his bedside: Sheriff Clarke. His uniform was slightly rumpled, the dark circles under his eyes betraying the stress he carried. When he saw Vincent stir, the Sheriff leaned forward, his gruff demeanor softening.

"You're awake," Clarke said, relief in his voice. "Tough, aren't you?"

Vincent tried to speak, but his throat was parched. Clarke poured a glass of water and brought it to his lips. Vincent sipped slowly, his mind racing as fragments of the betrayal resurfaced.

"Damien…" Vincent whispered hoarsely, his voice barely audible.

Clarke furrowed his brows. "What about Damien? We've been trying to reach him. His phone's been off, and when we went to his house, it was locked up tight. No sign of him anywhere."

Vincent's heart sank. He struggled to sit up, wincing as pain shot through his back. Clarke gently pushed him back down.

"Easy now. You're lucky to be alive, Kane. Whoever did this didn't hold back. You've lost a lot of blood."

Vincent gritted his teeth, his voice stronger this time. "It wasn't just anyone, Clarke. It was Damien."

The Sheriff's Reaction :

The words hit Clarke like a hammer. He froze, his face a mix of disbelief and confusion. "What the hell are you talking about? Damien Frost? Your partner? Are you saying he stabbed you?"

Vincent nodded weakly, each word a struggle. "Damien… he's the boy from the diary. The one whose family Augustus destroyed. He orchestrated everything—the murders, the notes. All of it."

Clarke leaned back in his chair, his face pale. He ran a hand through his hair, trying to process the revelation. "Are you sure about this, Vincent? Damien? That man's been your shadow for years. He's helped solve more cases than I can count. And now you're telling me he's the killer?"

Vincent's eyes burned with a mixture of pain and determination. "I didn't want to believe it either. But he told me himself, Clarke. He said it was revenge for what Augustus did to his family. He stabbed me, left me for dead. Damien's behind it all."

Piecing It Together :

The Sheriff stood abruptly, pacing the room. "This... this changes everything. If Damien's the one pulling the strings, we've got to find him. He's been ahead of us every step of the way, manipulating the investigation, covering his tracks. Damn it, Kane, this is a mess."

Vincent closed his eyes briefly, the pain and exhaustion threatening to overwhelm him. "He's smart, Clarke. Smarter than any of us gave him credit for. He'll be hard to find, but he's not invincible. There has to be something—some connection, some mistake we can use."

Clarke stopped pacing, his jaw clenched. "Don't worry about that right now. You need to focus on recovering. Leave the search for Damien to me and the team. But, Vincent..." He hesitated, his voice softening. "Why didn't you see this coming? You and Damien were like brothers."

Vincent looked away, guilt and anger warring within him. "Because I trusted him. I trusted him more than anyone. And that's exactly why he was able to do this."

A Break in the Case?

As Clarke reached for his phone to coordinate the search for Damien, a nurse entered the room, checking Vincent's vitals and administering pain medication. Vincent watched silently, his mind a whirlwind of thoughts and memories.

"Sheriff," he said finally, his voice firmer. "Check his house again. Look for anything—papers, files, anything that might give us a lead. And Clarke... be careful. Damien's dangerous, and he won't hesitate to hurt anyone who gets in his way."

Clarke nodded grimly, his earlier disbelief replaced by a steely resolve. "You just focus on getting better, Kane. We'll find him. And when we do, he'll pay for what he's done."

As Clarke left the room, Vincent lay back against the pillows, his body aching but his mind sharper than ever.

XXI

The Quiet Goodbye

Damien Frost sat in the dim light of a secluded room, his face shadowed by the brim of a hat that had seen better days. On the table before him lay a collection of meticulously forged passports, tickets, and a burner phone. Every detail of his escape had been planned to perfection. He had spent months covering his tracks, erasing his existence from every database and connection that could lead back to him.

The world thought Damien Frost had vanished, and he intended to keep it that way.

With a final glance at the contents of his bag, he zipped it shut. It was time. He stepped out into the cool night air, blending seamlessly into the crowded streets of a bustling city. By the time the sun rose, Damien Frost was gone—his destination unknown, his past life buried under layers of deception.

The World Moves On

As weeks turned into months, the search for Damien slowed and eventually stopped. His name became a ghost in police records, his face fading from the memories of those who had once worked beside him. The Darlington case remained unsolved, a chilling tale of murder and betrayal that the media eventually replaced with newer stories.

Vincent Kane, though haunted by the betrayal, forced himself to move forward. He had other cases to solve, other lives to protect. Damien's escape was a wound that never truly healed, but Vincent buried it beneath the weight of his work.

A Year Later

It was a quiet morning, the kind Vincent had come to appreciate in his otherwise chaotic life. The sun's first rays filtered through the window of his modest home, painting the walls in a warm, golden hue. He yawned, stretching as he made his way to the front door to retrieve the day's mail.

Among the usual collection of bills and advertisements was an unmarked envelope. The paper was thick, the handwriting unfamiliar. Curious, Vincent brought it inside, setting it on the dining table as he poured himself a cup of coffee.

He hesitated for a moment, staring at the envelope, before carefully tearing it open. Inside was a single folded sheet of paper. As he unfolded it, his heart began to race. The handwriting was deliberate, the words unmistakably personal.

The Letter

How are you, Vincent?

Your longtime friend, Damien.

Vincent's breath caught in his throat. He read on, each word cutting through him like a blade.

I'm sorry, Vincent, for hurting you. You know what? Though I left you that day unconscious in the rain, it was me who made the anonymous call to the hospital for an ambulance. That is why today you are alive—because of me.

You declared me a criminal, but don't you feel my side of the pain? Do you understand the agony of losing parents, of being alone in a world that didn't care? My actions may never make sense to you, but they were the only way I could find peace.

If possible, forgive me, Vincent.

The letter ended abruptly, without a signature or a return address. Vincent stared at the words, the coffee in his mug forgotten and growing cold.

A Silent Reflection

For a long time, Vincent sat at the table, the letter clutched in his hands. Memories flooded back—cases solved together, late nights at the office, Damien's quiet loyalty that had once been his anchor.

And then came the betrayal. The flash of the blade, the rain mixing with his blood as Damien whispered an apology and walked away.

Vincent closed his eyes, the weight of the letter pressing down on him. Forgiveness was a word that felt too large, too heavy. Yet, in the silence of that morning, he felt something shift—an understanding, perhaps, of the pain Damien had carried all those years.

He set the letter down gently and leaned back in his chair, staring out the window as the world outside began to stir. Life moved on, indifferent to the ghosts of the past.

In that moment, Vincent Kane chose not to chase them anymore.

OVERALL ENDING

Acknowledgments

Writing The Shadows of Darlington has been an intense journey, and I owe my gratitude to the readers who stayed with the story through its twists and turns. To those who believe in the complexity of human emotions and the gray shades of morality—this story is for you.

About the Story

At its core, The Perfect Crime, Almost is a tale of power, betrayal, and the lengths to which people go when consumed by pain and revenge. The Darlington family's grandeur masked its sinister secrets, and the bond between Vincent and Damien unraveled in the most devastating way. The story reminds us that the truth, though elusive, is never simple. It challenges the idea of justice and forgiveness, leaving us to ponder whether redemption is ever truly attainable.

Themes Explored

Betrayal and Trust: The friendship between Vincent Kane and Damien Frost is the emotional anchor of this story. Their relationship unravels in ways that challenge the very foundation of trust.

Revenge and Redemption: Damien's journey highlights how revenge can consume, while Vincent's struggle with forgiveness reveals the complexities of redemption.

Power and Corruption: The Darlington family's legacy shows how power can corrupt and destroy, leaving devastation in its wake.

The Human Psyche: The psychological intricacies of each character, particularly Damien and Vincent, bring depth to their actions, painting them as neither entirely innocent nor completely guilty.

Character Arcs

Vincent Kane: From a determined detective to a man burdened by betrayal, Vincent's journey is one of resilience and moral conflict. His ultimate choice to let go of his pursuit reflects his understanding of human fallibility.

Damien Frost: Damien evolves from a loyal ally to a tragic figure driven by loss and revenge. His actions, though reprehensible, stem from a deeply human place of grief and helplessness.

The Darlington Family: Their rise and fall are a cautionary tale of unchecked ambition and secrets that refuse to stay buried.

Key Takeaways

Justice is Subjective: The story leaves readers questioning whether justice was served, as the true culprit remains at large, cloaked in the shadows of unresolved truths.

Forgiveness is Complicated: Vincent's struggle with forgiving Damien mirrors the universal challenge of reconciling pain and understanding.

Secrets Never Stay Hidden: The Darlington family's downfall is an epitome to the inevitability of truth, no matter how deeply buried.

Final Thoughts

The Perfect Crime, Almost is not just a murder mystery—it is a reflection of the human condition, exploring the depths of love, loss, ambition, and vengeance. It challenges readers to grapple with the complexities of justice and morality, leaving them to draw their own conclusions about the nature of right and wrong.

As the story closes, Vincent Kane's decision to stop chasing shadows is not a surrender but an acceptance. Some truths are meant to remain hidden, and some wounds, though they heal, will always leave scars. Thank you for on this journey. May the shadows of the past remind us of the light we seek in the present